Treasure

of the

Ancient Wizards

By
Alexander Saunders

THG StarDragon Publishing

Printed in the United States of America.

For more information, to have letters to the author forwarded or any other communications, contact:
THGStarDragonPublishing@gmail.com
http://www.thgstardragon.com

THG StarDragon Publishing
Alexander Saunders C/O Teresa Garcia
PO Box 249
McCloud, CA 96057 USA

Book layout by Teresa Garcia
Final editing by Teresa Garcia
Cover design by Teresa Amehana Garcia
Cover conversion assistant Saorise Anderson

ISBN – Paperback: 978-0-9788028-7-5

First Edition: September 2023

From the Publisher

THG StarDragon Publishing is pleased to have become the new publisher for Alexander Saunders' books, and is looking forward to working with him in the future regarding other books he anticipates. As the story in this particular book was written when he was a child, great care was taken in preserving the voice while also looking over what his previous editor had polished his work to.

This company was started after my own difficulty in getting published in the early 2000s in order to help other authors with underrepresented voices. In those days it was authors from non-mainstream religions and child authors I noticed not having their works published as often. After my own son was diagnosed with autism it came to my attention that I needed to pay attention to neurodivergent authorship as well.

Submissions are always open, although only a few can be worked on in a year. Poetry, fantasy, spirituality, adventure, children's books... all are welcome. Child, teen, and adult authors are all valid. All stories deserve to be heard.

www.thgstardragon.com

About the Author

Alexander Saunders was born in Portsmouth England. His family later moved to Massachusetts, USA where he grew up, thus experiencing life on both sides of The Pond. He was diagnosed with autism when young.

His prolific writing, as a child and as an adult, is one of the things that has helped him cope with not only his autism but also some of the difficulties in his life. Like many others, and the characters in his fantasies, those hard times have shaped who he is. Writing allowed him the chance to use his imagination and to explore other possibilities. Like many, he has always had a particular love of dinosaurs. He, like many, believes that there is life out there on other planets. He believes that there may even be life on the other planets of our own solar system. This belief is one of the things that led him to write the books in his Dino Dimension books.

His hope is that you will enjoy reading his fantasies as much as he enjoys writing them. Please go to Amazon to follow his writing, or check the website of THG StarDragon Publishing for when his future books become available.

For now though it is time to gather around the library fireplace and listen to the storyteller.

https://www.amazon.com/stores/author/B07BJ28YN4

https://www.thgstardragon.com

Chapters

1

The Beginning

Hello, my friend. I am here to tell you a story, a story about an adventure my friends and I had in another dimension. Yes, I know you've probably heard so many stories like this before, but I am not so sure you've heard one like this. But in order to know more, you have to read on, and before I even begin, let me give you a quick background on myself. And yes I know in some ways people think it's strange to have yourself as one of the main characters, but like I said, this is a different kind of story and my way to escape reality since reality has never been kind to me.

Nevertheless, the life I had long ago is a life almost everyone has in these very bad times we live in, and many might disagree, but the reason these times are so bad is because we have a corrupted government, meaning we have politicians in the government who believe that taking from those who have nothing is a good thing, and it's why I had two working parents who did so much for me and my sister that they never had time to enjoy themselves. There were times we did, but as the corruption in the government got stronger and the rich were getting it all while the rest just struggled and suffered, those days came to an end. They just worked long hours with unfair and cruel management just to not only keep food on the table, but so we could have a place to live and, sometimes, what we liked from time to time. It made me see what the world is, and it made me so sad, I wished I could do something about it. But because I was so young and wasn't old enough for a paying job, there was nothing I could do, or so I thought.

I did find ways to help my family which were odd jobs for my neighbors, something my sister and I were able to do at a young age. These were jobs like yardwork, housecleaning, and even taking care of the neighbor's pets. It did us some good and we were quite a great team, but as time went by, my sister seemed to have more time for her friends and a social life than anything else that could help out and get ahead.

I worked alone, but soon that changed since I was coming to an age that no one likes or trusts. So in time, I began looking for a job, but in the meantime, I did the only money-making thing I could do in my spare time, which was to go around town and collect bottles and cans and redeem them for a little extra cash, and I know in some minds that is wrong. But in bad times, if you want to stay ahead or have a little bit for yourself, every little bit helps, which is why you should never throw away your cans or bottles. They can be the extra you need to help you through bad times, plus it's good to recycle because it helps the planet and ensures many that we can have a future.

But enough of all that. More can be said about that later; for now, let me take you to where the story begins. It was years ago on a bright clear summer day, and like I said, I was very young, and on days like this, I walked around town looking for thrown away cans and bottles. But I wasn't alone. I had a dog with me and he was a better partner than my sister. As we were on the edge of a small forest, which was usually the best spot to find empty cans and bottles, we saw there was nothing there, so today, my dog and I were just enjoying what we thought was just another ordinary day. It really was like any other day, peaceful and calm, until somewhere out of nowhere I heard a strange voice calling out, "Follow my voice, my child, follow my voice."

At first, I thought it was some punk trying to pull a prank on me, since a lot of people like to pull pranks on me, mostly my sister's friends. Plus, you should never do something like this if you don't know what to expect, because something like this always leads to something horrible. However, when the voice kept repeating itself, I left the shopping cart I used to collect cans and bottles, got a good grip on my dog's leash, and followed this strange voice.

I was ready for a fight, just in case what I feared was about to come true. As I kept following the strange voice, it led me right into the middle of the forest. When it finally stopped, I tried to see if I could find the source of the voice, but the only ones here were me and my dog. But as I kept looking, I soon saw a reddish, bluish light shooting up from the ground. As I kept looking at it, feeling shocked at what I was seeing, the strange voice called out and said, "Go to it, dig it up, and see what awaits you, boy."

"What do you mean?" I called back feeling a bit scared, and I really thought I was losing my mind at this moment, but when the strange voice said it again, it then said, making me feel more worried, "And understand it is something you need to know yourself."

And so, still feeling scared and confused, I tied my dog to the nearest small tree and started digging in the spot of the light with my own two hands. It was hard at first because I had to dig past dirt, roots, and rocks, plus a few minutes had passed in the process. When at last I found what was under the light I saw it was a large chest, a chest that was made out of rubies and diamonds, and I was curious to know what was in this chest, not just because it was a strange voice that had led me to it, but because nothing like this had ever happened to me before.

It took some time and some difficulties because the chest was so heavy, and I had a dog as well, but I managed to get the chest back and into the shopping cart and hid it under a lot of cans and bottles. I had to hide this chest because if anyone saw me with something like this, they would find a way to take it for themselves or ask me questions about how I got this and why I had it, and I was not going to say why or how, because no one would believe it. Plus, this chest would be worth a fortune, and even though I didn't do a good job hiding it, for some reason, the people I passed didn't seem to notice I had something hidden in my cart. But I didn't care; I just wanted to get it home without any trouble or any problems since the chest was making it hard to control the cart.

When at last I got home, I got a few bags from the garage, bagged up the cans and bottles I collected, put them in a pile with the rest I had collected that week, and sent the shopping cart to a hidden area. I then got the chest into my home and in my room without anyone noticing. Fortunately, there was no one in the house when I came home, which made me very happy. All the same, when I got to my room, the thing I was trying to do was find a way to open this chest. But there was no keyhole, no button, and no way to tell you how to open this thing up. However, just when I was about to give up, I leaned on the top of the chest and the middle part began to sink to the bottom. This allowed the whole top of the chest to disappear and showed me a lot of fascinating things, things that would even surprise you. These fascinating things were four old, large books with strange writing and symbols on the front covers, and a long thin red silver stick, which I knew at once was a wand. There was also a necklace with a strange golden key on it, but the thing that really struck my interest was a very old folded up piece of paper that said **Map** in silver writing on the center.

It was this old piece of paper I picked up first, and when I flattened it out, the word **Map** disappeared.

And new words began to appear all over this piece of paper, which was really amazing. Even more amazing was that it said in strange unknown writing,

> **Hello, future adventurer. What you hold in your hands is a map, but not just any ordinary map; this is a treasure map, but not to any ordinary treasure. The treasure you're about to seek is called the Treasure of the Ancient Wizards, one of the most ancient and only known treasures hidden in the Magicalworld. This treasure, as you're probably asking yourself, is one of the most valuable treasures in your or any other known world... so valuable that just a bagful of this treasure will make you rich beyond your wildest dreams, but to have it, you have to get to it first, which will not be easy.**

After I read this through a few times, still feeling shocked by everything that was happening, the words disappeared and what started to happen next was that the map began drawing pictures and lines all over the place.

Soon after that, a male voice, which sounded like the voice that had led me to the chest, spoke out of the map and said, "To start you off on your grand adventure, you must open up a portal at the exact spot where the map glows blue. There, it will create a link that will connect your world, which is the Humanworld, to the world called the Magicalworld. And once you've entered the Magicalworld, where the adventure really begins, you must follow the White Brick Path. This is the path which you must stay on at all times while on your journey and in this world, since it is this path that will lead you to the treasure, which will not be an all-day thing. All the same, the White Brick Path will lead you through the grass that is tall as trees, across the Long Wide Lake, and up the Great Mountains. It will then take you down and past Drainton City, through the Lava Ponds, and into the

Haunted Dark Forest. Once you pass through all these places, you then come up to a blocked up cave which you must blast through with a very powerful spell. Once in, you are to walk to the very end of the cave where you use the key on the necklace, and then you're there."

After the voice stopped, I looked at all the places and directions on the map and saw I had a long journey ahead. But soon, a battle raged in my head that was making me wonder if this was really a grand fortune. That would mean I would become part of the higher class, the very people I never had time for because of the way they are today. Nevertheless, I felt like someone really wanted me to have this treasure, and after the way I found out about it, I was all forth on doing this. When I was about to put the map away and get out the books, they magically came out of the chest. They then stacked themselves in a pile, and what happened next was this: Many letters began flying around my bedroom, and they then formed into words which now said,

Before you start on your adventure, you must read each and every one of these books. The reason for this is because they'll help you tell the dangers you'll be facing in the Magicalworld, and this might take some time, but there is no rush; that treasure isn't going anywhere. And as time goes by, you'll be allowed to tell the people you trust about all this, but don't tell everyone, or they'll be after what is yours to find.

A few years had now passed since I found the chest, and through all that time, once I got used to the fact that I was able to do magic, which I was given the second I touched the wand that very same day, I spent a lot of time in my room, but not all the time, because I had to come out to do some chores, use the bathroom, get something to eat, and—which is the part I never liked—be forced to go to school, something I never enjoy, especially with how schools are in these times. Nevertheless, from everything I've learned from the two books called **How to Learn Magic Yourself** and **The Great Big Book of Spells**, I've been using magic a lot. Sometimes, to help me get my chores done, or duplicated the cans and bottles to make some extra money to get some fast food, caused some of my favorite snacks to appear when I didn't want to get them myself, and even caused some extra money to appear in my parents' wallets when they needed it.

But the most fun part about using magic was causing my sister's friends to leave when they wouldn't stop coming around, because they were always coming over even when my sister promised they were not. During these problems I had with my sister I not only used some magic to cause her some grief like I thought she was giving me, but also used some spells to cause problems for my sister's friends. I didn't do this all the time, because it says on the first page of **The Great Big Book of Spells**, "Don't use magic to solve all your problems or show off; always use it for the right reasons and when you really need it."

Of course, I did disobey this rule from time to time because magic was a real help in my life, but I hoped to have a lot of it when my journey to the treasure began. Also, when I read these books, which I spent day after day reading, they sometimes read themselves, which only happened whenever I got stuck on a word or when I was too tired to read myself. And a lot of the times when I read these books, they got stuck in my head, which I didn't know at first, but every time I forgot what I read or what I had learned from these books, they magically made me read them again so I wouldn't forget and would understand what I would or would not do in the near future.

But right now, the book I was reading was called **The History of the Magicalworld**, which I found to be a very interesting book, and for the past two months, I had tried to see if I could find anything about the Treasure of the Ancient Wizards. This was because I wanted to know more about what I was in for, and when at last I found the page, this is what it said:

Long ago, ten witch sisters and ten wizard brothers wanted to prove to the

people of the Magicalworld that our dimension was not the only one that existed. They wanted to prove there might be others, even ones that can't do magic or can't live forever. Everyone thought they were crazy because it was impossible to exist without magic, and there was no such thing as death. But these twenty witches and wizards didn't care; they just did it, not just to prove a point, but for the fun and adventure. Rumors over the years have said they did find this world and saw that people were not so different than how they are in the Magicalworld, but with some of the things they did, they became rich, so rich that they transported their fortune to a cave chamber they all knew and sealed it, and it is this chamber that many have avoided and protected for all time that has passed. Over the years, they

became richer and richer and started to show off their skills and magic in that world. When they were revealed, they made a run for it since they were in a world where people fear the unknown. When they used so much of their magic to get back to the Magicalworld, nineteen of them burned out and died. And the one they say is still alive was never seen again, and no one knows to this day where he is.

After I finished this page, I wondered, but then a voice in my head said, "Now is not the time to think about it." After that I then took another second to wonder what my life would be like once I found the Treasure of the Ancient Wizards. I began to fear that I would become the same way so many rich people are today: greedy, self-centered, and not caring about how those who work for a living are suffering. Just as all this formed in my head, the same voice then said, which was the same voice I can't stop hearing ever since I found the chest, "You will not become the very thing you hate the most, and more will be revealed to you in time. But for now, focus on getting to the Magicalworld before you focus on the next step."

And so I obeyed, and before I go on, I want to just say something which I should have said before. That is, don't always listen to voices in your head unless it is for a selfless deed or for something good because there are always two sides, and the one you should always listen to is the good side. But of course, sometimes if you listen to the voices in your head, people will think you're crazy. But getting back, after a few more years had passed and I finally finished the last of these books, I then spent a lot of my time looking for the spot which was the spot where I could open a portal to the Magicalworld. This was very important because I needed to know where I could go if I wanted to start this adventure.

Through all the time I was looking for the spot to start this the voice from the beginning was helping me. I was glad about this, too, because it was only his voice, I could hear when it spoke and guided me. And it didn't bother me one bit, because those who loved to pick on me couldn't bother me, and I was picked on a lot in school. And most of the time, they enjoyed tormenting me about a past I want so much to forget; however, I did find out that a lot of these punks said things like:

"What is wrong with him?"

"It's like he's hearing things."

"Do you think he's going crazy?"

"There must be something wrong with him."

"He needs to see a doctor."

I didn't care, because I knew when all this was over, I'd be living the good life, the life almost everyone deserves. After two and a half months of searching, I finally found the spot and it was in between two trees in the school courtyard. This was bad because this spot was in an area where I could easily be watched, but then I remembered not everyone looked in this area most of the time. So all I had to do was come up with a good plan to do this without anyone seeing me do what no one would ever believe seeing.

A few weeks after I found the spot, I thought the time had come to tell my four best friends about all this, from the day long ago when I found the chest all the way up to the spot where I had to go and enter this world to find the treasure. Also, the names of my four best friends and the greatest people I ever had in my life are Marvin, Andria, Talia, and Eddy. These are people I trusted more than anything, and they've been there for me ever since my sister and I had a falling out.

And it's why I trusted them with anything and why I wanted them to know about all this. What they looked like was this: Marvin was tall and thin and had jet-black hair, and he was the one who loved to have a joke. But when the situation was serious, he would be there and help no matter what or how hard it was. Andria, however, was short for her age, had highlighted hair, and was the smart one of our group. As for Talia, she had long, dark hair with a clear face and was one of those who always smiled; basically, she was the heart of our team. And Eddy, he may not have looked it, but he was very strong and had a round face and short hair.

Let me just say that these are not my friends' real names, and the reason I changed them is because it was the only way I could add them in this story, but the only name I didn't change was my own. Yes, I know in some minds that might not be a smart thing, and yes, I know I did it in another book. But since I'm narrating and one of the characters, I thought, why not? Plus, it made this more fun to write.

But now as I take you back to the story, the second I told them everything about the Treasure of the Ancient Wizards during free period in school, they did not believe me. This was something to expect because no one in their right mind would believe something like this, and as far as many are concerned, magic does not exist, and we were at an age when no one believes in it. But when I showed them the map and used some magic to turn a pencil into paper, refilled our teacher's coffee mugs, and caused a few snacks to appear for us, they were shocked and surprised, and even said things like,

"I can't believe it."

"This really is real?"

"And you're really going to do this?"

"And no one knows but us?"

I felt uncomfortable hearing all this, so I said, "Yes, I'm going to do this. Also, I don't know how long this is going to take me, but I'll try to tell you."

"Wait!" my friend Andria cut in. "Aren't we coming with you?"

Hearing this made me feel uneasy, because this was the last thing I was hoping for, which was why I now said, "Guys, this is going to be a very dangerous quest. I can't let you risk your lives for something like this. It's why I'm doing this alone."

"But Alex!" my other friend Marvin began. "We've always been there for you through everything in our lives."

"I know, but…"

But just before I could finish, we noticed something happening to another piece of paper. At first, everyone thought I was doing it, but when a note appeared on the paper, this is what it said:

Alex,

Let your friends come with you on your journey to the treasure, because they have earned that right as they have earned your trust over the years. And no, my young friend, you don't have to do this alone; you never had to be alone most of your life. And if all five of you work together on your journey to the treasure, nothing can hurt you. Also, my boy, it is time for you to put your leadership skills and your friendships to the test. But the last thing to say to you all is, the whole time you are on your journey, you must all believe in magic. For as long as you all believe in magic and believe in yourselves, the things you will face will not be a problem, and it will make everything a little easier.

After we all read this through a few times, the words disappeared and my friend Talia said, "Alex, what was that?"

I chuckled a bit before saying, "Just the source of whoever wants us to go on this treasure hunt."

All four were glad I said this, and what my friend Eddy said was, "Does that mean we're all going?"

I said "Yes," by nodding my head, and the excitement almost drew the attention of our teacher. But after that, we all began to plan on how we were going to do this and when we were going to do it.

2

The Adventure Begins

The end of the school year was finally here, and it was on this day we were going to leave this world, meaning this was the day we were going to start our journey through the Magicalworld to find the Treasure of the Ancient Wizards.

The reason we chose to do this at the end of the school year was because we didn't know how long our adventure was going to take, because like I said before and what I told my friends, this was not going to be a one-day thing. Also, since everyone in the school, all teachers and students, were so desperate to get out as fast as they could, we had less of a chance of being noticed until it was too late. Another reason we chose this day was because it took me a while to pack and buy all the things we needed for this adventure.

The things we were taking with us were a lot of food packed in a very large cooler and a large tent which belonged to my parents, but they hadn't used it in years since we didn't go camping anymore. We also had five camp beds, a few pillows and blankets, and, in case it was too cold in some of these areas, very heavy sleeping bags, along with five very large sacks. These sacks were for the treasure when we finally reached it, and I gave the other four to my friends when we came to school that day. Also, I had to be very careful when doing all this, because no one could know but myself and my friends.

I still couldn't believe I was able to afford all this, and the reason I say this is because the day after I said my friends could come with me, I was in a stump because I realized I needed money to pay for the things we were going to need for this adventure. And I couldn't ask my parents, not without telling them what

I was about to do. By the way, you should never keep secrets from your family, especially when it comes to something like this. But then again, this is something they wouldn't believe, and even if they did, they might try to stop me, something I did not want. I will say I wanted my sister to come, but since she was with a new crowd of people and was not good at keeping secrets anymore, I couldn't. But on that same day, when I was trying to find out how to get everything my friends and I were going to need, the voice in my head said, "Go to your phone and check your email." So I did, and the second I opened my email app, I saw an ad message saying,

I am looking for valuable items and will pay a grand price and not ask any questions.

I saw that the place was not that far away from my house, so after seeing the address and seeing that one of the items this person was looking for was the chest that started it all, I then hid the chest in a huge trash bag and said I was going out. As I was halfway there, I thought this was not a good idea, and I almost turned back when the voice told me to keep going.

The person I sold the chest to was a very rich man who rented the place I went to for a few days and was looking for things to buy for his collection, and when I showed him the chest, he said, "Boy, I've been looking for something like this for a very long time, so…"

He paid me a great amount in cash since he saw I was not old enough to cash in a check. Also, I thought there was something strange about the man, like I'd seen him somewhere before, and just when I was about to leave, this same person said, "Whatever you hope to find, you may find more of what you hope, because sometimes in life, we find more than what we hope for, even if you weren't looking for it in the first place."

I didn't know at the time what he meant, but I soon put it out of my mind as I went to the store to buy a few gift cards to my favorite online store, and it was at this online store I bought everything I needed. Of course, I had to be very careful because I couldn't let my family know what was coming, and since there were people over all the time who were people my sister likes being around I had to keep so much hidden, plus a few months back, some of them had stolen a few things. Since they were always forgiven, I needed to be very careful.

Getting back to the present part of the story, the other things we had packed were a lot of clothes, which was the only thing I told my friends to remember to pack, and, if they wanted, their own food, pillows, blankets, and sleeping bags, since I wasn't sure I had enough for us all. Everything we packed was in five large rucksacks, including my books, which were in my own, and five days before this started, I gave the other four rucksacks to my friends so they could pack what they needed and more.

One more thing to say is that the only things I kept on me at all times were my wand and map, which were both in different pockets, and my key necklace, which I had around my neck. In fact, ever since I had this, I never took it off except when I had to sleep.

What we did when we came to school on this day, which I should have mentioned before, was hide the rucksacks near the school courtyard. I even put a spell on them so no one but us could see them and they would only become visible when they were picked up and on our backs. This was so we had them ready when the time was right, and the reason we didn't bring them in the classroom was because our teacher might start asking the very questions we didn't want him to have the answers to.

Now, in most of my stories, I make teachers the bad guys because of the experience I had in my own schooltime, but this is the exception, because this teacher was a wise old man and might be one of the only good teachers of this time. However, if we brought the rucksacks into the class, he'd begin asking questions. And because we knew how good he was at getting the right answers, he would find out in a second what we were up to. And as much as we hated lying to him since he was the only good teacher we ever had, we didn't want him to find out or stop us from going on this adventure, which he would do if he knew our parents didn't know all this.

When the school day was almost over, our teacher told us and the rest of the class to line up at the door, and we went to the back of the line since this was part of our plan. Plus, being in the back of the line is a good way to sneak away when no one is looking. Nevertheless, our plan was a simple one: While everyone was so focused on getting out for the summer, we could sneak away, get to the school courtyard, and open the portal to the Magicalworld, and this could finally start.

When we were out in the hallway, we saw our chance and went down another hall. We then got to the spot where our rucksacks were hidden, and the second they were on our backs, they became visible. And after making sure we had everything, which only took a few seconds to do, we went out into the courtyard. As we did this, I took out the map and began looking for a second time where it glowed blue. And when it did, we looked around to make sure we were not being watched, and then I put the map away, took out my wand, and said this spell:

"Portalless, openess!"

And at that second, a rainbow-like hole opened up in front of us and we all walked in. And the second all five of us walked through the portal, it sealed itself, and what we saw, which I know I've said a few times before in other stories, is a sight you have to see to believe. And the reason I say this is because we were looking at the most wonderful and fantastic things probably no one in our world has ever seen before or will ever see in any lifetime. Everything around us was so beautiful: The grass was so green and fresh, it was like it was cut and watered every day. The sky was much bluer and more wonderful than the one in our world; even the clouds were wonderful. As for the sun, it was much smaller and younger than the one we know so well, and the smells, oh, the smells! These smells were so great, it was impossible to get sick or even sneeze; in fact, it was like breathing in youth and wonder at the same time. But after a while, we had to draw ourselves back to reality, but before we did, we looked back and saw a distance leading to who-knows-where and a horizon in that same distance. As much as we would have liked to see what was there, the only horizon we needed to focus on was the one leading to the treasure. So at that second, I stowed my wand away, got out the map, and began to see where we had to go from here. The map said we needed to stay on the White Brick Path which we were standing on at that very second, and after we saw this, the map caused new words to appear that now said,

Hello, adventurers. You have just entered the Magicalworld, home to creatures you have only heard about in fairy tales in your own world.

However, this is no fairy tale, and this world is just as real as your own, but you'll know more about that as time goes on. For now, it's time to get started on your journey to the Treasure of the Ancient Wizards.

But first, you must follow the White Brick Path to the grass that is tall as trees, but once there, beware of werewolves.

After reading this through, I was hoping to read more, but these words disappeared and were replaced by directions on where to go. I was disappointed at first, but I guessed more would come as we traveled on; however, just when I was about to put the map away and begin the long walk, my friend Talia said, in a nervous-like voice, "Alex, what are werewolves?"

At that question, we stopped and I got out my wand, then used it to get one of my books out of my rucksack. This book was called **The Book of Magical Creatures, People, and Places**, which I had read a few times over the years. But as I had it hover into the air, I used some more magic to flip through the pages, and when at last it came to the page I was looking for, the book landed in my wand-free hand, and it showed us a picture of a creature which had the arms and legs of a human, and the body, hands, feet, head, tail, and fur of a wolf. And what the top of the page said, in four-inch-long writing, was "Werewolves!" And at the bottom of the picture, it said,

These are very wild and very dangerous creatures. They live in small caves, long grass areas, and lighted forest. Though they kill anything that comes in their territory, they are afraid of loud noises.

After we all read this through, my friends were shocked, and what my friend Marvin said was, "I thought werewolves were what people turn into on a full-moon night."

"Oh, that's just a myth!" I said as I shut the book and used magic to put it back in my rucksack, and then I went on and said, turning to them all, "Nevertheless, when we reach that area, not only do we have to be very careful, but also, we all need to stick together."

"Why?" they all said together.

"Because!" I began feeling a bit annoyed. "I'm the only one here with magic and knows all the spells that might keep us alive."

When they all agreed to this, we walked on, and the adventure to the treasure really began. We all enjoyed this walk because it was doing us a world of good, and when we were eight miles away from where we started, we saw a lot of phoenixes flying through the air. I knew what they were, which were large birds that looked like streaks of fire flying in the sky. I told my friends what they were, even told them what the creatures were that had just stampeded in our sight and blocked our path for a few seconds. These creatures were bright white horses that appeared out of nowhere with long, sharp horns on their heads. As the unicorns were galloping in the opposite direction, I told my friends that they travel in herds like this to protect themselves, and when they were gone, my friend Andria asked, "You think we'll see many different kinds of creatures on our journey to the treasure?"

"We might!" I said with a laugh. "There are so many different kinds of creatures in this world, but not all of them are friendly. And some of them, mostly the wild animals in this world, eat things like us." I knew I spoiled the moment, so I went on and said, "But the worst we can run into right now are werewolves." The second I finished this, we came right in front of the grass that was tall as trees. And standing right on the left side of the entrance was a sign in purple writing that said,

Beware of werewolves.

At that, I took out my wand and said in a worried and scared-like voice, "Follow me and stay close." And as we walked through this grass, we were amazed at how big it was, because no normal grass can be the size of trees. Nevertheless, all seemed calm and peaceful until I started to see movement in the grass. I knew we were being hunted, and just before I could do or say something, ten or twenty werewolves jumped out of nowhere and surrounded us. These werewolves who had a hungry look in their eyes made sure we couldn't escape. And it reminded me of how regular wolves catch their prey, and I would have been fascinated by this if we had not been the prey. We were all scared; I was the most, and just when we thought all hope was lost, I remembered a very powerful spell that could save us. So I raised my wand to the sky and said with all the force I could manage, "Exploredcon Toloring!"

And at that spell, a loud noise like five bombs going off at the same time blasted out of my wand. And all the werewolves started to make a run for it, and the second they were gone, I lowered my wand and said to the others, "That's taken care of, so we should…"

I never got to finish what I was trying to say because I noticed my friend Talia was shaking and still in shock, and when we all tried to calm her down, she said, still shaking as she spoke, "That was… That was, so, so scary!"

I felt guilty and responsible for this, so I said, hugging her as I did so, which she returned, "Talia, it's over; they're gone, but if you want to go back, I'll—"

"No, no!" she cut in, and then she went on as she backed away, "I want to come, really, I do. Anyway, the five of us have done worse than this before; why should this time be any different?"

This was true, and we all laughed at this for a few seconds, which caused a few cubs to appear and run at the same time. And if you think I'm going to go into details about the things my friends and I did in the past, you're wrong. Because one, it is not what this story is about, and two, I don't want you to think we are a bunch of trouble-making treasure hunters. When we finally got out of this grassy area, which took a while to do, we stopped five feet away just so I could get out the map, and what it said now was,

Now that you're out of the grass and away from the werewolves, you must follow the path to the Long Wide Lake and cross over to reach the Great Mountains. But as you cross the lake, be very careful, because you might end up as prey for the sea serpent.

After this disappeared my friend Eddy said as I put the map away, "Did the thing just say 'sea serpent'?"

"Yes!" I said as I gave him a serious look. "It's a giant monstrous-like snake that lives in large waters."

"Oh!" Eddy said again. "That's good to know!"

"Eddy, are you afraid of snakes?" Marvin teased.

"Just the really big ones." And then he told us about the time when he saw a really big snake in one of the greatest movie series in history. Based on one of the greatest reads that are still enjoyed to this day, he's been afraid of really big snakelike creatures ever since.

I felt a bit bad once again when he told us all this, and the thing I said to him, hoping this would help, was, "Eddy, you need to face your fears, because we're in a world where anything is possible. Also, after seeing creatures no one in our world has ever seen or believed in, we need to be ready for anything and not be afraid."

This allowed Eddy to say, "I understand, Alex, and I will try my best to be as brave as I can if we run into this serpent. I promise."

"Good," I said with a smile on my face, and then I went on by saying, "But that's not a promise I need just from you, Eddy, but from all of you." And when they all understood this, I went on and said, still feeling bad and a little nervous as I spoke, "And if worst comes to worst, then I guess I'm up for a challenge I knew would come when I read about them."

"What are you talking about?" Andria asked me with a scared look on her face, which allowed me to say, ready for the reacting as I spoke, "What I mean is,

I'm going to have to fight it if it comes at us or tries to do what the werewolves almost did."

And to that, they all said in loud voices, which scared another werewolf trying to attack us again, "Are you crazy?"

"Maybe!" I said before any of them could say another word. "But as I said before, I'm the only one who has magic and knows the spells that will keep us all alive."

"But Alex!" Talia began who was about to continue when the others said at the same time, "What do you mean?"

"What I mean, guys," I said feeling a bit worried, "is that the day you all said you wanted to come, I started practicing spells of defense because I knew we were going to need them." The second I finished, everyone was silent, and when I saw that no one was going to speak, I then said, "This is because I didn't want anything to happen to any of you, but right now, let's get out of here." When they all asked why, I pointed in the other direction and said, "Because I see three more werewolves coming this way."

And after I used the same spell I had used before, we walked on because we were not in the mood to see any more werewolves. When at last we reached the lake, we were surprised by what we were seeing, because this lake was like looking out into the ocean. This lake was larger and wider than any lake you would see in the Humanworld with waves splashing onto the sand. This was kind of cool to see, but not as cool as seeing the sun sparkling on the water; again, this was a great sight to see for anyone.

As much as I didn't want to spoil the moment, I still saw a problem, and the problem was that there was no way to cross this lake. Plus, the path ended the second we came in sight of the lake, something I was not counting on. I never like it when a good thing turns bad, but it felt like we came to a dead end. However, just when I was thinking we should rest for a while, even see if we should spend the night here, Andria and Talia called out from a distance, "Guys, we found a way across!"

It turned out the second we came here, they wandered off for a few seconds to see what this place was like. And it was a good thing they did, because the more I looked around, the more I thought this was not a safe place to spend the night. All the same, when we caught up with them, we saw that they found a very long, wide land bridge which was our way across and allowed us to press on.

As we began to walk across, I got out my wand and said, "Let's try to be as careful as we can, and with any luck, we might not have to deal with the sea serpent." And so we walked across, and everything seemed fine like it was when we passed the tall grass area, but then I said, "Shh, you hear that?" The reason I said this was because I started to hear movement in the water, and even one of my friends thought they saw something moving nearby. And when the others heard it, too, and saw a large shadow in the water, they almost panicked. However, the movement in the water soon stopped, and what I said now – trying my best to keep calm – was, "When I say run, run!"

Just before I could give the signal, the sea serpent appeared out of the water and attacked. What this beast looked like was this: It was the mix between a cobra and a python, and even had the head of a rattlesnake. But it was the size of three school buses and blue to match the water we saw. And when it was about to strike with its long, sharp, pencil-like teeth, I was ready for it. When its mouth was wide enough, I pointed my wand at it and said, "Firest blastercon!"

A great burst of fire blasted out of my wand, and the sea serpent swallowed that instead of us. It wasn't enough, though, and before it came back for a second attempt to kill us, I said to my friends as I got ready to fight, "Run, get out of here, save yourselves!" But they didn't leave me, and they said things like,

"No!"

"We're not leaving you!"

"We're staying with you no matter what."

"If you go down, we all go down."

I was glad and worried at the same time when I heard them say these things. Even though they were not going to leave me while I fought this beast, it didn't stop me from worrying that they might die with me. But they were standing by my side, encouraging me to keep fighting this serpent, and I tried every spell I knew on this creature. But all I seemed to do was make it angry, but most of the time, it was to buy some time so we could get to the other side. Unfortunately, the serpent kept coming back for more, and at one point, we thought it was gone. But it came out and blocked our way to get to the other side and tried to chase us back to the beginning. As it was snapping its jaws, I tried more magic to fight this thing, but it was immune to the magic I was using on it. But just when I thought there was no other way to fight this creature, I said a very strong spell, which was, "Bladeico, slasho!" And what happened next was a sword-like blade shot out of my wand and slashed the sea serpent from head to tail.

This lasted for at least a minute until it fell back into the water with a loud splash causing all of us to get wet. I felt very guilty for what I did because I never wanted to kill this creature; I only wanted to drive it away. When my friends saw the look on my face, as I stowed my wand back in my pocket and led them away they started to say,

"You had no choice!"

"It was the only option you had left."

"If you didn't kill that thing, it would have killed us."

"And none of us are in the mood to die."

"Thanks, guys, that really means a lot," I said feeling a bit happy. Five minutes later, we came to the very end of this land bridge onto what might have been another land or continent. I thought it would take longer, but I guess a lot of running from the serpent would do that. But we didn't care about that, because it only meant we were another step closer to where we were going, and after a while, we saw that we were in range of the Great Mountains. However, as we looked ahead, we saw it was starting to get dark, which was why I now said, "All right, we're stopping!"

Our timing couldn't have been better, because this spot we saw was a good clear spot off the path. There was a small brook of water a few seconds away and a few trees for good cover, but me saying this surprised my friends, which was why my friend Marvin said, "Why are we stopping?"

"Well," I turned to them and said, "if you look up into the sky, you'll see it is starting to get dark, and I don't think we should be traveling at night... especially since a lot of dangerous creatures come out at night in this world, creatures that are almost as dangerous as the ones we faced today."

"So we're staying here?" Andria said.

"Just for the night," I said, looking around. "Anyway, this looks like a good spot to stay."

"So what do you want us to do?" Eddy said.

"While I set up the tent and everything else, you guys go look for some firewood, but please don't go too far," I said.

And so, after we got our rucksacks off our backs, they went off and I took out my wand and cast a few spells to set up a campsite, even a few spells to ensure we would not be attacked in our sleep. I know this is being lazy, the part about using magic to set up a campsite, since I knew so much about camping from my father. But like I said, it had not been used in years because of a few problems my family were having. This is mostly because of the path my sister took, and I wish I could have stopped that, but because I was preparing for this day. I never did, which is why I sometimes blame myself for every bad thing that has happened.

As I sat alone for a few seconds, this area reminded me of all the campsites my parents took me and my sister before life was starting to affect everything, but those happy memories and grand moments reminded me why I wanted to do this in the first place. True, it was an unknown voice that led me to the very thing that started all this, but I hoped one of the things to do —once we reached the treasure, that is—was have those great times again before it was completely too late. But then I remembered it is never too late to enjoy life; you just need good timing, something times like this had caused to stop.

As I was remembering the grand times I had before things got worse and my family could not afford to go anywhere anymore, I wondered if they even missed me or knew I was gone. I say this because for a short time before this all began, they seemed to always be there for my sister when she caused more problems and I felt like I was nothing to them, but I put that out of my mind and used the magic I had to set up a good place to stay for the night.

When at last I was done, my friends came back with a lot of wood for a good fire, and after they dropped the wood into the hole I made by magic, I then said, "Firedest, burndome!" And at that, a fire began to burn, giving us some warmth as the night sky began to appear, and when the fire was settled, I got five pizzas out of a cooler, placed a grill I had in my rucksack on the fire, and began cooking everyone some pizza. The second they were done, I placed them on some paper plates and we all started to enjoy a great bite to eat.

As we were eating, we also looked around and saw how beautiful the area was at night. We even saw a few wild animals in the distance and were grateful none of them ate meat or we'd be prey. But as we were finishing our dinner and I used some magic to turn the trash into water for the fire, we began talking about how this day had been, and it allowed my friend Andria to say, "Well, guys, this has been a really exciting day."

"What makes you say that?" I said with a laugh and taking a bite at the same time since I was not finished, but what she said after throwing her plate in the bucket I had caused to appear for the trash to turn into water was, "Well, Alex, first you scare off werewolves, then you kill a sea serpent—I mean, what's happened to you?"

"Yeah, what has happened to you?" Eddy put in as all of them asked this same question, which caused me to laugh a little at this.

When I was able to speak, I said, "Well, guys, as I learned how to use magic, a lot of skills came with it."

We all laughed at this, and then, after a few minutes, we all did some thinking on what we wanted to do once we found the treasure. Also, and I knew this was coming, too, they all started asking me how long this was going to take, and the answer I gave them was, "We still have a long way to go, guys."

"How long?" Talia asked.

I replied, "We still have to travel through the Great Mountains, and it will take just a month or more just to get all the way to Drainton City, one of the magical cities of this world, and then there's still the Lava Ponds and the Haunted Dark Forest."

"So this is going to take a while," Marvin said, which allowed me to say, "Guys, I did warn you about that."

"Who says we're complaining?" Marvin said again.

"Anyway," Talia began, "this will all be worth it once we reach the treasure."

"That is true!" Andria added on, and just when we were about to have another laugh or change the subject, Eddy then said, "Can I ask a question?"

"Go ahead," I said turning to him just as he said, "Well, even when we do reach the treasure, how are we going to get home in the aftermath?"

At that, I said, "Well, my plan is to open a portal in the treasure chamber once we get as much as we can take and hope we land somewhere close to home."

"You think that will work?" Marvin said.

"I hope so, I really do. If not, we're going to have to find a phone and make a call."

"Makes you wish you didn't tell us to leave our phones behind," Andria said in a teasing voice.

"We kind of had to. But let's not worry about that now, because we have a long way to go, so we'd better get some sleep."

They all agreed, and so, after I put out the fire with the water I turned the trash into, I made sure we were safe and followed the others into the tent. In the tent, we all found huge areas to sleep in, and just when we were all about to go to sleep, something else was mentioned, something I was hoping was not going to be brought up at any point on this adventure. All the same, they asked me why we didn't get to bring our phones with us, and the answer I gave for the second time was, "Guys, we are in another dimension, and I didn't think we could take the chance that they might do something that might get us killed or explode on our travels."

This is what I said a few days before we did this, but the real reason I didn't want us to bring our phones was because I didn't want to take the chance they would work and we would get nonstop calls from our families trying to get us to come back or nagging us for what we were doing or calling us at times that we may run into danger. All the same, after making sure a few things were in my rucksack, I got into my sleeping bag, and after we all said our goodnights to one another, we all went to sleep.

3

The Great Mountain Journey

The next morning, I woke up before the others did because I thought I could use some time alone and to see where we had to go next. It was still dark and the sun was starting to rise, but I didn't mind because I had nothing to worry about. Nevertheless, after I got out my wand, I gathered up some more wood and then started a fire with the same spell I had used the previous night. I then got out the map, and when the fire was burning and giving a good light, I looked down at the map, and what it said now was,

You are now away from the lake, and you're lucky that the sea serpent didn't get you, even luckier there was just one because with a pack, it would have been your end. But your next challenge before you reach the Treasure of the Ancient Wizards is the Great Mountains. Traveling through the mountains will take you a month or longer just to reach Drainton City. But getting there will not be easy, for as you go up and through the mountains, you'll be facing a lot of dangers beyond your wildest imaginations. You can avoid most of them if you read this map very carefully and avoid a few paths that will not lead you to where you want to go, meaning there will be paths that will confuse you and make you think you're going the right way but will only lead you to your death or a fate worse than death. So if you focus and listen to the right directions, then

you'll have nothing to fear and you won't have to get to the top to reach the other side. But again, if you don't pay attention, the only thing you and your friends will find at the end of this adventure is your deaths.

The second I read the last words, the map then showed me yet again a lot of places and directions on where to go. And as I began to read on, I saw a few odd things, and the oddest thing the map showed was a building that looked like either a mansion or manor. When I asked in my head, "What is this place?", one of my books, which was **The Book of Magical Creatures, Places, and People**, zapped out of my rucksack. It then landed on my lap and started flipping its pages until it stopped at a page at the far end of this book. This page had a picture of a very strange-looking manor house, and on the top of the page, it said, in large and fancy writing,

The Magical Mountain Manor

And below the picture, it said,

This manor is home to a lot of magical outsiders who all live in peace from the rest of the magical society. It's a great place for long wandering and tired travelers to rest before starting off again.

Reading this made me feel uneasy because it reminded me of a story I once read a long time ago. This story was about three travelers on a mission to find a lost prince of a grand magical kingdom. As they neared their destination, they soon got sidetracked by two strangers and forgot about their mission. They then came to a place they thought was good and wanted nothing more than to stay, but then saw they were going to be eaten by the giants that lived in that place. This was almost like that same situation, which is why I knew this had to be a place to avoid completely, because I didn't want us to end this adventure the same way those three travelers almost did.

When the others woke up to the smell of cooking bacon, sausages, and eggs, we all started to eat a good breakfast and enjoy a beautiful morning. The sun was now high enough for there to be light, and we all enjoyed the first morning in another world. When at last we were done eating, I made what we didn't eat turn into water and allowed it to pour into the brook. After that, we all took turns going into the tent so we could change into a new set of clothes. I then used some more magic to pack the whole place up. And once we made sure we had everything and our rucksacks were on our backs, we set off once again.

It wasn't long until we made our way to and through the Great Mountains, and as we traveled, we noticed, which was very hard not to do, how wonderful and amazing the sights we saw were. In most mountains, you'll see lakes, forests, and fields of meadows, and that is what we were seeing and more. And most of these areas reminded me of more campgrounds and areas I used to go to when I was young, but cleaner and more beautiful than you can ever hope to see, and how much I wish I could explain properly, but you might lose your mind if I even try.

Plus, it was kind of hard to really go into details about what nature is like in this world. A few days had passed, and as we were crossing a fast-moving stream, one of us nearly fell in, but luckily, they were saved by the others. The second we were across, I turned and said, as I saw the stream getting rougher, "Well, guys, I told you this was going to be tough, but—"

"If you're going to ask us to turn around and end this right now…" Talia said with a stern voice.

"Think again," Andria added on.

I wanted to say something, but then Marvin said, "Yeah, Alex, plus we made it this far, didn't we?"

"But guys, we still have a long way to go," I said before anyone could say another word, and just when I was about to continue, my friend Andria said, "So what? We wanted to come, and we'll continue this until we reach our destination."

I knew I was not going to win because when it comes to things like this, my friends always have the final say and outnumber me at every turn, and that's why we pressed on, but not for long. After a few hours, we came to an area with a lake and so many trees surrounding the area, and it allowed me to say, "Guys, as much as I'd like to keep going, we're going to stop here for the night."

They, too, noticed it was getting dark, and I thought they were going to say something, so I just said, "Guys, getting to this treasure is not going to just take a few days, and since this is a safe and good place—"

"We get it," they all said, because even they saw this was a good cover for us. But we noticed this was a place where we could have a swim, even catch some fish for a good dinner, which I did with some magic, but as I was fishing and in a deep part of these waters, too, I noticed something big coming this way. Believing that it was another sea serpent, I made a swim for it, but then the thing came out of the water and revealed itself to be a man. But this man had a fishtail instead of legs, and the thing he said to me in a stern middle-aged voice was, "What's your rush, boy?"

As shocked as I was, I was still able to say, "I thought you were a sea serpent."

The merman laughed and then asked why my friends and I were here, and the answer I gave the merman was, "We're just travelers, and we're only

spending the night here, but if we knew this area was
—"

"Oh, don't worry," the merman said. "I just wanted
to know; we all wanted to know since we began to see
fish flying out of the water."

"We'll put them—"

"Oh, don't do that, lad," he said patting me on the
shoulder. "Fish are food, and if you and your friends
are really spending the night here, you should enjoy
how good fish are."

"Even take some with you when you leave," a
mermaid said when she came out of the water, and that
very night, we not only had a grand meal of fish, but
we were also joined by the merpeople of this lake. It
was a fun night, and they enjoyed how good fish taste
when they're cooked. In return, they ensured we had
enough for the next days to come, even showed us a
few areas to take to get to the other side of the
mountains.

Days soon turned to weeks, and already we were
nearing the top areas of these mountains, and through
that time, we escaped a lot of dangers we almost
walked into. But we were still alive, and we soon found

a few more shortcuts that led us to quicker and easier ways through the mountains, and it was not just shortcuts that were a big help to us, but paths that were like train turntables, and what you had to do was wait three minutes on these things until they stopped you on the right path. It was fun because it allowed us to see a few more grand sights the mountains had to offer.

Also, and this is something I should have said before, we were lucky we were still alive, because some of the things we faced didn't like seeing things like us. But I'm getting ahead of myself in this story, so let me bring you to the first thing we came to.

A few days after that fun night with the merpeople, we came to a small village that looked like something from the settler eras. And the first thing I realized was that this might not be an easy pass, which was why I said to the others while I looked at the map, "Wish there was another path we could take."

"Why? What's wrong?" my friend Marvin said while looking a bit worried himself.

"Because," I said, putting the map back in my pocket, "that's the village of the ghouls, and ghouls hate any non-ghoul creatures in their areas."

59

"So what are we going to do?" Andria asked with a scared look on her face, but to her answer, I got out my wand and said, looking at the many ghouls going in many directions, "Stay close to me, and with any luck, none of them will notice us passing through, plus most of the time, any ghouls that pass usually cause trouble, so…"

How I knew this, is something to save for another day. As we walked through the village I was worried that something bad was about to happen. And the second this thought came into my head, we came to the heart of the village, and this is where everything went wrong. I say this because just as we were passing an area with a group of teenage-looking ghouls, they looked at us suspiciously.

Just when I was about to say something, one of them began shouting to the whole village, "Freaks, freaks, freaks! Evil magic in the village! Evil magic in the village!"

We soon heard other ghouls saying,

"Get them, get them!"

"Find them and kill them!"

I didn't know what these teenage and adult ghouls meant when they said what they said, but when many began saying, "Get them!" and, "Find them and kill them!", all five of us made a run for it.

As we ran, we saw we were almost at the end of the village, and it was a good thing, too, because a lot of these ghouls began shooting arrows at us, even used what looked like burning torches, but the fire was green, and we weren't in the mood to see how badly it could burn. And as we got to the end, a few of them got us in the legs and almost shot us in the heart, but luckily, I was able to use a healing spell when it got serious.

I also ended up fighting a few of these ghouls but did my best not to kill or even fight the women or children. The reason I fought to defend was because if I killed any of them then that would prove what they were saying was right. But as much as I wanted to go easy on them, they were putting up a really good fight. Because they wouldn't let us pass in peace, I had no choice but to fight and even kill a few just to get out of this village.

Once we were a good few miles from the village, I performed a few more spells which not only healed us and allowed us to walk again, but also allowed us to press on to reach the treasure. And no sooner did we put enough distance from the village we came to a mountain edge and saw walking through it was not going to be easy. But it was the only way forward, and as we walked, there were a few times when the edges were too narrow to walk on. This allowed me to use some magic to help, and when we got a chance, we saw a few creatures like dragons in far-up areas and a few large griffins flying through the air.

We soon came to a cave that was hard to move through, but luckily, it was not that long, and the second we were out, we came to another village. This new village was not like the one that almost killed us, because they let us pass in peace, plus it had a mixture of many different magical creatures and didn't mind strangers like us passing through their lands. This was not the only good village we passed in the great mountains; we passed many as we continued our adventure, and a lot were a great help, especially when it came to getting to another area.

After passing and traveling through more areas and lands in the mountains, we came to a hill-like village, and just as we were about to pass, an innkeeper, which was a female faun, came up to us and said, "Would the five of you like to come in for a bite to eat?"

As grateful as we were for this offer, our problem was that we had no way to pay, and when we mentioned this, she said with a smile, "The five of you look like you've come a long way, so whatever you get, it's on the house."

Now we were grateful, and for the next few hours, we enjoyed what was a feast instead of a meal. We were almost asked to stay the night, but unfortunately, that was something we had to pay for. After we were done eating, we said "Thank you" and continued on our journey to the treasure.

One thing to say before I continue with this story is that in these times, it is almost impossible to get a free meal. But on the rare occasions when it does happen, always be grateful for it, because it might be the only one you'll ever get.

The day after this, when the morning became the afternoon, we came to a large, wide trench, and I knew we were about to have a headache when we came to this area. And just when I was about to say something, it happened: A loud, deadly scream, too intense to describe, echoed, not just in the trench, but all around us; in fact, it was so loud, we thought the whole mountain could hear it. However, it only appeared for a second and was gone, but soon it was back and was louder than ever, like there was more than just one. It stopped again, and what my friend Andria said, feeling both worried and annoyed at the same time, was, "What was that?"

"A banshee!" I said, Eddy then said, as the sound came again, "What's a banshee?"

When it stopped again, I got out **The Book of Magical Creatures, People, and Places** and began flipping through the pages. When I finally found the right one, I soon cast a spell to block out the next scream from the banshees and, at the same time, showed my friends a picture of a creature that looked like a large bat, mixed with a monkey with gray stripes and black all over. I was just about to say something, but that was when the scream came back worse than before.

The spell I used was a temporary spell, meaning it only lasted for a short period of time. But I cast it again and said as everyone looked at the picture of the banshee, "Banshees are giant batlike creatures that have a deadly scream that will give you something worse than a headache. They are never seen, but you know they are there when they begin to scream. They do not sleep, but travel by night to find other areas to scream."

After this, we all agreed we were not going to wait until dark to get through this trench. So after I cast the spell for who knows how many times, we pressed on.

The farther we went, the more times I had to cast my spell, which began to annoy the banshees. I say this because their screams, as we soon found out, were not just to give their victims a headache. There was more to it, because when we got to the end of the trench, two banshees blocked our path. This was a shocker because they're never seen, and just when we were about to do something, these creatures screamed us off our feet and sent us flying a foot away from where they were. As we tried to get back up, they kept us down; it was like they did not want us to leave.

When I saw a chance, I cast a spell that not only scared the two holding us down away, but also all the banshees in the trench. I would love to tell you how many we saw, but I lost count after a few seconds. When the banshees were gone and we all got back up, I heard Marvin say to Andria, "Wish we could do that."

A few days later, we packed up the camp bright and early in the morning since the area we spent the night at was a rocky area. But we had no choice since the next clear area would take us until midnight to get there. Just when we were about to leave, we were attacked by a group of ogres and trolls. We knew what they wanted to do as they formed a circle barrier so we couldn't escape, because I once mentioned that creatures like these—not all of them, that is—like to rob and kill travelers, and seeing that this group was not so bright, I then said, "Look, we don't want any trouble; just let us leave in peace and no one will get hurt."

The ogres and trolls laughed at this and one of them, which was a troll, said in a mean grunt, "Oh, someone *will* get hurt, boy, if the five of you don't hand over all your valuables and—"

"We don't have any!" I began as I got out my wand. "Now, let us leave in peace or else."

At that, they began to move in for the kill, but I was too quick for them, because at that moment, I cast a very strong and fast spell which not only caused these robbers to lose their large clubs they had for weapons, but also to sink into the ground. And as they sank deeper into the ground, I started to feel sorry for them, so I allowed their heads to stick out of the ground so they could breathe.

The ogres and trolls were not happy about this, and what many of them began to say now was, "Let us out, let us out!"

And what I said to these robbers as we set off once more and were laughing at what had just happened was, "I don't think we will."

"You look better this way anyway," Talia put in as she shot a smirk at them.

"Now you can't hurt anyone anymore," Eddy finished up as he aimed a kick at one of their fat heads. It was a good thing he missed, because it was wrong to hurt someone when they were already down. By the way, the reason I did not tell you what these creatures looked like is because there are already too many stories about ogres and trolls already. And if you've read those stories before, you already have a good picture in your head of what they look like. Plus, they're really hard to explain like almost every creature is in this world.

Getting back to the story, I thought ghouls, banshees, ogres, and trolls were the worst of it, but I was wrong. Because four days after we encountered the ogres and trolls, we came to a long, dark cave tunnel which would take us to another part of the mountains and hopefully a bit closer to Drainton City. But this dark cave tunnel was full of dark creatures I can't tell you about, or you might not want to read any further. I lit my wand before we went in, and just when we were a few steps in, it happened: We were attacked by many dark creatures, creatures we could see and ones we could not. Some even caused Andria and Talia to scream, and I had to use a lot of magic just to get us through this tunnel. I even had to kill a few, but fortunately, after getting a few away from us, I cast a spell which caused a light so bright, it kept many other dark creatures from attacking us.

When at last we got out of the tunnel, we were badly beaten, scarred, and bleeding in a few places. And after I used a lot of healing spells, we were back on our feet in two seconds, and that's when I said to myself, "Magic really is the most wonderful thing in the world."

My friends were saying this, too, because we all knew without magic, we would be dead by now. No sooner did we get away from that tunnel than we came to an area full of quicksand. We knew it was quicksand because when I stopped to tie my shoes, both Talia and Andria went ahead, and the next thing we knew, they began to sink in the sand. When I saw this, I used a spell to get them out, and as grateful as the two of them were, it didn't stop us from seeing we had another problem, which was how to get across an area of quicksand. This was when I got out **The Great Big Book of Spells** to find the right spell, which was on page seven. However, this was another temporary spell, so after I cast it and the sand turned to solid rock, we ran as fast as we could until we were clear from this area and saw no more quicksand. After that, we thought we had it easy because the next two days were clear.

We saw more areas of the mountains and crossed over a few that were connected by wooden rope bridges. There were a lot of these as we traveled, and most of the time, I wondered if some of them could take our weight. But as things began looking good as we journeyed through another part of the mountains where many trees, brooks, and rivers came in sight, we noticed storm clouds beginning to form. I brought umbrellas for this, but I was not prepared for how bad it was about to get.

The rain that started was not ordinary rain. It wasn't even flood rain. It was just rain too dangerous to travel through. The raindrops also felt like being poked so many times; even our umbrellas were not enough to keep us dry. I even tried to use some magic, but even that was not enough, and soon we couldn't even see where we were going. Fortunately for us, there was a cave up ahead, and we all made a run for it, almost slipping off our feet a few times just to get there. However, the first thing we did as we entered was make sure this cave did not belong to anyone. But it looked like no one had lived in this cave for a while, and after looking back outside, I managed to cast a spell to ensure no water could get in. After building a fire, we began to listen to how strong the storm was getting and how much rain was beginning to fall.

Even though this cave was keeping us dry and safe, it didn't stop the rain from pounding the cave walls, and as the days passed and the storm was getting worse, thunder began to join the storm, making it hard for us to sleep at night or even think, and because the thunder was so loud, we were shocked the cave wasn't struck by lightning. As more days began to pass and we gathered around the fire, I said in a sad voice, "I knew there was something I was forgetting to prepare for."

"Oh, come on, Alex!" Talia began. "You can't prepare for everything."

"She's right!" Andria put in. "How were you supposed to know a storm like this was going to hit? You know as well as we all do that weather is unpredictable."

How true that is, because that seems to always be the way, especially when you are out and about. All the same, as we all fell silent, I began to pass around something for us to eat.

As we ate, my friend Talia said, "Still, we're safe in this cave and this storm can't last forever. Storms never do."

"I hope you're right, Talia," I said as the storm began to get stronger and stronger. "I really do."

It took some time, but when at last the storm was finally over and the sun began to shine into the cave, we were able to set off again, but we took it a bit easy just in case another storm was on the way. As the days went on, we soon saw we had another problem, a food problem. Yes, we were almost out of food, which was bad because we were nowhere near Drainton City. And as we all noticed how short our food supplies were getting, I tried using a few spells to double up our food, but all it did was make it vanish. I even offered to cast a no-hunger spell on my friends like I did to myself a few times. But they didn't want a spell like that cast on them; in fact, the more I did it to myself, it did more harm than good.

A day later, tensions began to rise, and what my friend Andria said, feeling both arrogant and frustrated, was, "Is there a place around here that can give us some food that will help us get to our destination?"

I got out the map at this, and just when I was about to say there was no chance of it, my friend Marvin said, "Guys, look here: The map says we're not that far from a mansion which says we can stay a while. Maybe they can give us some food and even let us rest for a few days."

When they were all for it, I mentioned what happened in a story we all used to read, the story about three travelers who did the same thing when they were on a mission to find a lost prince, and it made my friend Marvin say, "Alex, that was just a story."

"And we're in a world–" I cut in, feeling a bit of anger rising up inside of me. "Where all those stories might be real due to the countless times we were almost killed. The last thing I want is for us to become a feast in a place like that." I stopped because I hoped that settled the matter, but when they tried to disagree with me, I then said, "I know we need food, but do any of you really want to end this adventure the same way those three travelers almost did?"

"Then what do you suggest we do?" Talia ground out.

"Well!" I said feeling so frustrated. "I know you guys are going to hate me once I say this, but the best we can do is save our food until we get to Drainton City and see if we can get some food there."

"That's your idea?!" Andria flipped-out.

"It's either that or get eaten ourselves," I said in a voice that could be heard from miles around. However, everyone was mad at me for doing this, and that night, when we found a good place to spend the night, none of us spoke, which I expected, and that was why I didn't try anything to change the subject. But I did warn them things like this would happen. I also wondered if I was doing the right thing. But I didn't want to put my friends in even more danger than we were already in.

Because of this silence, I was afraid we might not live to reach our destination. None of us slept well that night, and the next morning, we all woke up to the sound of chopping wood. We were afraid to know what was out there; nevertheless, when I got my wand and got out of the tent, I was ready for anything, or so

I thought. Because the second I was out, I was stunned and surprised at what I was seeing. I was looking at a centaur, a half-man, half-horse creature. What this centaur looked like was this: He had a long, black beard, long hair, and a black horse body.

When he saw me, he said in a polite English accent as he put down his axe and walked up to me, "Good morning to you, sir. Forgive me if I woke you. I'm just gathering some wood for my home."

I was shocked at what I was seeing and hearing, and just when I was about to say something, he said as my friends came out of the tent, "I see you're not alone, good sir. Two young ladies and two strong gentlemen with you. Such an honor, such an honor. We don't get many travelers in these areas; in fact, many never stay in an area like this or live the way you five do."

A few seconds of silence followed this, and then my friend Andria said in a stern but worried voice, "Who are you, sir?"

The centaur laughed when she said this, and then he said as he moved his axe by a tree, "Oh, yes, I'm sorry, I forgot to introduce myself. Oh, where are my manners these days? I must admit a centaur at my age does forget a few things from time to time, but still, my name is Comdust."

We all thought this was a strange name, but we were in a strange place, and so, after getting over that, we all said at different times, "Pleased to meet you, Comdust."

"And pleased to meet you all," he began with a bow. "And may I ask what your names are so we all know who we are?"

And so, after we told him our names, he thought they were all strange names from the look on his face, but after a second of silence, he then said, when he saw us getting some stuff out of the tent, "My new friends, will it be okay if I join you for breakfast?"

It was this that made me say, "Oh, we're sorry, Comdust, we would like you to join us for breakfast, but—"

"But we're starting to run out of food," Marvin said.

"And we're trying our best," I said again, "to save as much as we can until we get to Drainton City."

"Drainton City!" he said in surprise. "That's a long way from here, a very long way indeed. And you'll starve to death before you get there. We can't have that, now can we?" Silence fell for a few seconds, and that's when Comdust said, after coming out of a deep thought, "Tell you what: Why don't you all pack up your stuff, and after I've gotten the last of my wood, I'll take you to my home, which is the Magical Mountain Manor that's only a few miles from here? And there, we can all have a great breakfast, something I think we all need. What do you say?"

Everyone except me was all for this, and when Comdust noticed the look on my face, he said, "Is there something wrong, Alex?"

This snapped me out of a deep thought and allowed me to say, "Oh, no, it's just that we're strangers and—"

"Oh, I see what you're thinking, boy," he began in a stern voice and before I could finish what I was saying. "And no, my new friend, I am not leading you or your friends into a trap or anything bad. The place I'm taking you all is a place where you can all rest for a while and have grand feasts and meals whenever you want. And if you wish to stay for a few days, since you could use some time to rest, my friends will give you a warm and comfortable place to sleep in the main house. When you are ready to leave, we'll make sure you have everything you need and more, I swear."

Hearing all this not only reminded me of how the three travelers got sidetracked from their quest, but also of how many other stories like that were of someone being promised the same thing only for it to end in a bad way. But since I didn't want to be rude, we agreed to go, but it didn't stop me from being worried. When Comdust disappeared, I cast a spell to pack up our area and all our stuff, and at the same time, we got our rucksacks.

Comdust appeared with a wheelbarrow full of wood and said at the same time, "Now that we're all ready, let's go."

As we followed him, I noticed we were being led away from the White Brick Path, and I didn't like that one bit. And it started to make me think my worst fears were about to come true, and I hated what was happening in my mind as I believed the worst. But all this disappeared when we came to the biggest and widest mansion we'd ever seen. But then again, my friends and I had never seen a manor's main house before. This place was just like my book described it, but bigger than it was in the picture. The whole manor house was bright blue, had a lot of windows of all sizes, and looked like it covered the whole top of this area of the mountains.

When we came to what looked like the biggest door ever to exist, Comdust left his wheelbarrow on the side and then went to the door. He then reached out his hand to open the door, and a doorknob appeared in his hand, and we all went inside. The second we were inside, we saw a grand sight before us. I say this because we were looking at a very large room filled with stairways, doors, and portraits of other places in the Magicalworld. Unfortunately, we didn't have that much time to enjoy this, because the second we were in, Comdust told us to leave our rucksacks by the door and that someone would handle them later. He then led us through the manor and all the way to the kitchen.

The second we entered the kitchen, we were like we were every time we came to a new place in this world, amazed at what this kitchen was like. Nevertheless, this kitchen had tables and chairs of all sizes and everything you needed for cooking, even places to stow away food, which were the biggest things here. When

Comdust had us all seated, he then went to another door and called out as loudly as he could, "Wendy, Wendy, come in here! We have breakfast guests!"

"I'm coming, Comdust," a female voice called back which sounded very young. "Just don't rush me."

In two seconds, a witch came into the kitchen, and the reason I knew she was a witch was because she was wearing a red witch's hat and had a wand in her hand. She also wore a set of dirty robes which happened to be garden robes. We guessed she was working in a garden before Comdust called her in; however, the thing he said to the witch now was, "Forgive me for interrupting your morning gardening, Wendy, but you're the only one awake and available to perform the breakfast spell for our guests, and the reason I can't is because—"

"I know you're not a wizard, Comdust, but who and what are your visitors?"

At that, he turned to us and said, "You know, that is a good question and something I should have asked when we met."

I was afraid of this, and just when I was about to say something, Comdust just said, "What are you guys? Are you tall leprechauns, or elves without—"

"We're nothing of the sort," Talia cut in. "We're humans!"

These were the last words I wanted her or any of them to say if we ever came to a situation like this. However, the second Talia told these two what we were, both Comdust and Wendy began to laugh like crazy. When we asked what was so funny, Comdust just said, "I'm sorry, but that is impossible; humans don't exist."

"They are just a myth and legend," Wendy added who finished up by saying,

"What are you, really?"

When Talia said it again, they laughed even harder, and when she showed them some proof, they stopped laughing.

After a few minutes of silence, they forgot all about this, and then Wendy said, waving her wand a few times, "Fooder, western, arms!" And at her spell, all the plates, bowls, goblets, knives, forks, and spoons of all sizes started flying all over the kitchen. The second a few of them landed at the tables, food of all kinds, but different from the food we had in our world, began shooting out of the plates and bowls, and strange-looking drinks appeared in the goblets and fine-looking glasses. We all thought this was good when we began to eat, and it wasn't long until we were not the only ones enjoying a good breakfast.

Five minutes after we started eating, all the people who lived in this manor came in to eat. There were not that many, and what we saw were five giants, which brought a few fears into place, a family of elves, three leprechauns, and a female centaur who was Comdust's wife along with four other centaurs. There was also a small group of minotaurs, a few hags, nymphs, and three satyrs. I thought that was all until we saw a small group of witches, wizards, goblins, brownies, and a vampire couple.

My friends thought this was kind of cool to see many different people live together like this. But I still felt like this was not a good place for me and my friends to be. I was not going to say anything about it yet, but I did begin thinking that something bad might happen the longer we stayed in this place.

When the people who lived here realized we were in the room, and after Wendy and Comdust told them what we were, they thought we were very fascinating creatures, as we did them. When some of them began asking us where we were from, how we got here, and why we were here, we answered every question except the last one, because I didn't think it was a good idea to let them know we were here for the Treasure of the Ancient Wizards. The others agreed with me in case it brought some uneasy situations into play or trouble that I told would happen if we got too close to anyone we met while we were in this world.

All the same, when everyone ate as much as they wanted, a wizard with dark gray hair and beard got up and said, "Anyone want to go hunting?"

At that, a giant, two minotaurs, three centaurs, and one of the vampires got up along with a brownie, three goblins, a nymph, a satyr, and two witches.

The wizard said with a smile on his face, "Well, then, let's go."

And before you could say another word, they were gone, and the second they were gone, I told my friends who looked full that we should go, too. It took a while for them to agree, but when they did, we all got up, and when we were almost out of the kitchen, a voice from behind said, "Where do the five of you think you are going in such a hurry?"

The one who spoke was a giant, a very old giant, and what I said to this, hoping it would help, was, "We think we should leave now, because we still have—"

"But you can't leave!" the old giant said again.

"That's right!" Comdust said then saying, "The five of you barely have enough food and drink to last you to wherever you're going, and you can't survive like that."

"Comdust is right," the old giant said again. "You can't survive with the amount of food and drink you have."

"That's why you should stay with us until we restock your supplies," Wendy began. "We'll even give you some extra clothes to take with you as well when you are ready to go."

My friends agreed to this, but I still felt uneasy, which was why I said, "You really would do that for us?"

"Of course."

And so, that made us stay, but that's what made me very worried, and I wondered if this would be the end of us all.

4

The Great Visit and the Dream

Everyone **but** myself was enjoying themselves at the Magical Mountain Manor. While my friends were either wandering around the manor eating really good food or talking to the people who lived here, I was outside sitting on a huge boulder by the mountain edge reading the map and looking at the sights. I saw a chance when one of the elves began giving us a tour of the whole manor. I didn't really want to stick around, so when I saw a hall that was another way to the back of the manor house, I went down it, went through a door to the back side of this manor, saw a boulder, and just sat there worrying and wondering.

86

I had a good view of the other end of the mountains; it even gave me a great view of Drainton City and some really grand sights. And even though I was on the far top of the mountain and the city looked like a speck from where I was, it was still a great sight.

I ended up sleeping in my sleeping bag on the grass that night, and the next afternoon, when I was looking at the map, I asked it, "Where would we be right now if we didn't stop here?" And the answer it gave said we would be at a different part of the mountains right now, meaning we would not be any closer to Drainton City and we would have run out of food by then. This did upset me more; in fact, I was planning on continuing alone, but I did not want to leave my friends. If I left them here and my fears came true, it would be my fault, and I could not live with myself if anything bad happened to them, but I also believed something would if I just stayed out here.

"Alex!" a voice from behind said, which almost caused me to fall off the boulder, but I just jumped in surprise. However, when I turned around to see who spoke, I saw that it was the old giant my friends and I met when we came here. The giant was walking toward me, and when he saw he got my attention, he then said, "Is it okay if I sit here with you?"

"Go ahead," I said feeling uneasy, but I didn't want to be rude. However, when he sat on my left, he caused the ground to shake, but I was prepared for it, and after I put the map back in my pocket, silence fell. Before I go on, let me say that this is almost like the same situation in another one of my books. But it was the only thing I could come up with in a situation like this, plus sometimes moments like this can help with what is to come, and we can learn something we never thought we needed to learn in the first place.

Getting back to the story, after a few seconds of silence fell between the giant and myself since we were waiting for someone to talk, of course I had nothing to say, but the giant, on the other hand, did, because after a few more seconds passed, the giant looked around and said in a fatherly and wise voice, "I must admit, my boy, you picked a good sight to see: not only Drainton City, but the pride part of the mountain areas."

I didn't know what he meant, but then he directed my attention to the left side of the mountains and I saw what he meant. It was a beautiful, bright-colored valley with large waterfalls, streams, and so much more. And just when I was about to get the map back out and see if we'd get to pass it if we ever left this place, the giant then said in a kindly voice, "I see you're enjoying this, and these are great sights. I should know; I come out here a lot to gaze, not just at all the wonders of these mountains, but because it is a good place to think and be alone. However, that's not the reason I came out here, lad."

I turned to him when he said this just as he turned to me and said, "I came out here because I think there is another reason you've been out here." He waited for me to say something, but when I didn't, he said, "Ever since you and your friends arrived, you've just distanced yourself from us all, which is why I'd like to ask what's troubling you. But I think the best thing to say to you is, I know what's troubling you."

I was not surprised to hear this, but I didn't want him to know that, so I said, trying to look a little surprised, "You do?"

"We all do!" the giant said again. "Your friends told us everything, even why you came to our world in the first place."

The second he said this, I turned to the direction of the mansion and said to myself, feeling very angry at the same time, "I knew I never should have brought them."

"They only told us," the giant said as if he knew what I thought, "because we were all starting to worry about you."

"But why?" I said, trying to be polite. "You don't even know me."

"That's not the point, Alex," the old giant said with a smile on his face. "But the reason we were starting to worry about you was because you've only eaten once since you've been here. You've been out here since yesterday, and the only reason nothing came at you, since a lot of wild animals come to this area at night, is because a few of us stayed up all night just to protect you."

That is something I never mentioned, but the previous night, when I was sleeping, I thought I heard strange noises. I thought I was just having a bad dream.

But hearing him say this made me wonder a few things, and just when I was about to say something, he went on and said, "We know the reason you're out here is because you don't trust any of us, and that is something I would like you to tell me about."

I felt like I was being lectured, something I never liked even when I was young. But it made me see that I might have made a mistake in my judgments, so then I said, when I looked up into the giant's face, "Being here reminds me——"

"Of a story you once read in your own world," he cut in, finishing my sentence at the same time, which allowed me to say, still feeling a bit worried, "Well, yes, and how did you know about that?"

It took a while for him to say anything, but when he did, I thought there was a bit of disgust in his voice as he now said, "Your friends told us about that story, which I and the other giants here found to be an insult to our kind." I wanted to say something to that, but he went on and said, "But that's not the point, lad; the point is, we know you and your friends faced a lot of dangers. But you did encounter a few good people as well, like the innkeeper who gave you a free lunch when you passed her village."

I asked how he knew about that, and he just said, "She's a friend of ours, but what I am really trying to say to you, lad, is that you are safe here. Because you were not told the way to get here by an evil witch and a knight; you were led here by our friend Comdust, and there are not just giants living in this manor. Others live here, too, and we have no plans of making you and your friends into a feast. We do a lot of hunting, so why eat those who have come a long way? Plus, it's wrong to eat guests."

After he finished, I said in a sad and shameful voice, "I am so sorry."

"That's all right, boy," he said smiling down at me. "This is just what happens when you believe in the wrong stories or get told the wrong things." We both laughed at this, and then he got to his feet and said, "But let's drop all this, because the hunting party should be back any minute now, and you look like you could use a bite to eat."

So after I got on my feet, we both walked back to the mansion, which was only a mile from where we were. And when we both walked through the kitchen door, the old giant said after he got everyone's attention, "Look who I brought back, everyone."

"Oh, at last!" Comdust began with a chuckle.

"I thought he was going to stay out there for another night," a witch wearing red said who went on by saying, "And if he did stay out there, I was not going to keep the werewolves away from him again."

"Well, I had a talk with him," the old giant began. "And now, he's ready to enjoy the welcome his friends have had since they arrived."

The second he finished this, my friends came into the kitchen, and when they saw me, they started saying things like,

"So you've finally decided to come in, have you?"

"I thought you'd never come in."

"I'm surprised you're still alive!"

"I hope you learned something from this!"

At this, I said, not just to my friends, but to everyone in the kitchen, "I'm really sorry for what I did and for not trusting—"

"We already forgive you, dear boy," another witch said before I could finish. "But we'd better not catch you by that boulder again."

We all laughed at this, and after a few seconds, another witch said, "Also, Alex, one thing we want you to do tonight, after you've had something to eat, of course, is take a bath, because you smell like five ogres on hot days. Multiple days in one."

Everyone laughed again, even me, and just when we were about to stop, there was a bang from the other door. What came through it was the hunting party, and what they started saying, holding up their kill as they spoke, was,

"Look how many unicorns I killed today."

"See how many dragons I got."

"I caught four griffins and five Pegasi."

"I caught us a large sphinx."

"See how big this basilisk is."

"See these giant spiders I got for us to eat."

"But look at this chimera I got for us."

"Well, this means," a hag began just as she walked into the kitchen, "we can feast another night."

But the hunting party wasn't listening to the hag, because they had just realized I was in the room. And the looks on their faces were enough to show they were surprised, and what one of them said, who was a wizard with a brown bushy beard and spoke in a stern manner, as he came up to me was, "Well, I see Mr.

Lonely has finally decided to stop being a brat and come in, haven't you?"

At that, I wanted to say something to this wizard, but the old giant stepped in and said in a stern voice, "The reason he finally decided to come in is because I had a talk with him, and now he knows he can trust us as his friends do."

"Well!" the brown bushy-bearded wizard said again. "It's a good thing you have that effect on people."

"I'm glad I do," the giant nodded and went on by saying, "Anyway, I don't think Alex wants to die before he and his friends reach the Treasure of the Ancient Wizards, isn't that right, my boy?"

"That's true!" I said feeling a bit upset and going on by saying, "And even if we didn't stop here, my friends and I still have a long way to go."

"And some of these areas," another giant said, this one female and cooking the caught food as she went on, "are not that easy to get past since some of the villages that are located in the far areas of these mountains are just as bad as the ghouls you faced. But don't worry yourselves; that treasure you're after is not going anywhere."

"Anyway, boy," a minotaur said, who almost looked human except that he had a bullhead, and fur, and armor for clothing, "you're the only one who has the key to get into the chamber where the treasure is kept, isn't that right?"

"True!" I said feeling the key by my chest.

"Also, Alex," the brown bushy-bearded wizard began, "why are you and your friends so desperate to have the Treasure of the Ancient Wizards anyway?"

"Because!" Andria began, and like the others, she was quiet the whole time this was happening. "It can be very useful to us in our world."

"And the times in our world," Talia put in, "are very hard, and we can use some of the treasure to help make a lot of lives easier."

"That is one of our main goals!" I began. "But we do plan on living the kind of life you guys have and give our families everything they deserve. But another reason we're doing this is because I think someone wants us to find this treasure."

"What do you mean by that, boy?" the old giant asked.

It took me a while to say this, but when I was able to speak, the thing I said now was, "On the day I found the chest that gave me everything I needed to know about the Treasure of the Ancient Wizards and this world, it was a voice that led me to the start of all this."

At that everyone began whispering, and what Comdust now said to me in a worried and serious voice was, "Alex, what did this voice sound like?"

And so, after I described what the voice sounded like, they all started whispering things like,

"You don't think it was him, do you?"

"Impossible."

"He was destroyed with his other brothers and sisters long ago."

"But they say he's still alive somewhere."

"Then how come he hasn't shown himself or allowed us to know he is okay?"

"What are you guys talking about?" my friends and I said together.

"Oh, nothing!" Comdust and the old giant said together, and this allowed me to say in a stern way, "It just sounded like you guys don't—"

"It's not that," the old giant said knowing what I was about to say, and went on by saying, very clearly feeling a bit sad as he spoke, "It's just that we knew those witches and wizards."

"You know them," I said in surprise with my mouth hanging open.

"You didn't tell us," Eddy said in the same tone as mine.

"That's because," one of the vampires said. "we thought this was something Alex needed to know."

"Well, I'm glad you told me," I said, feeling a little disappointed. "But how did you know those witches and wizards?"

"Because this place is their home," Comdust said.

"You're kidding!" my friends and I said together.

"Oh, no, we're not," the old giant put in. "This manor was their home for many years, and when they started welcoming outsiders like us to live here, it was proof that they were the best this world had to offer."

"And it was a sad day," Wendy added, "when we heard what happened to them."

Hearing this made me sad, why I now said as I went through my pocket for the map, "This treasure is rightfully yours, so—"

"No!" the old giant said before I could finish, going on by saying, "That treasure is nothing but a living reminder of the family we lost, and if you want it, you can take it."

"Try to take it all," one of the centaurs said who finished up by saying, "Because that is never going to do anyone any good sitting there."

"Are you sure?" I said feeling a bit uneasy, and what the giant now said as food began to appear on the tables was, "Yes, I am, but right now, let's just enjoy a grand dinner before bed."

As every one of us began to eat, one of my friends, which was Marvin, said, "So now you know we can trust these people, right?"

I nodded at this since my mouth was full of food and I was not in the mood to eat and talk at the same time. However, the thing my friend Talia said after she took a bite of her meal and spoke in a stern voice was, "What I still don't get is why you never bothered to look in that book of yours called **The Book of**

Magical Creatures, People, and Places before you judged these people."

It took me a while to speak because I was trying to cut up a piece of meat, which happened to be unicorn meat. After cutting it and sending it down my throat, I was able to speak, and what I said was, "Well, like I said to all of you before we came here, this place reminded me of what happened in a story the five of us used to enjoy a long time ago. Also, after being attacked so many times by many different creatures in these mountains before coming here, it made me think we had to take some precautions, and I did not—"

"Are you forgetting," Eddy put in, "that we did meet some good people on this adventure?"

"What are the five of you talking about?" a nymph said that just come over to see if we had anything extra or if we'd like something. However, she asked again what we were talking about, and we mentioned the village we had passed a while back, and she then said, as we gave her some of the food she asked for, "Where did this happen?"

And as we told her this, one of the satyrs said, coming over as well to put a few extras on our plates,

"We know that faun. She's an old friend and she enjoys giving free meals to those who deserve it. You five must seem likable to her."

I then said the giant had mentioned her to me, and that allowed the nymph to turn to me and say in a motherly voice, "But all the same, you were willing to trust her but not us."

I was just about to repeat my answer when the old giant came over and said, helping me out with this situation, "How about we all agree he was just worried about his friends' safety? Plus, as we all know, this is a dangerous world, which is why we all live in this manor: so we can live in peace and away from the savage society living beyond this area."

My friends and I felt sorry when we heard this, which was why we now told them that we were outsiders in our own world. And it allowed a female centaur, who was Comdust's wife, to say as she came over to offer something big to eat, "And none of you have a place to go like we have?"

"It doesn't work like that in our world," Marvin began. "Even when it almost does, it always gets destroyed since nothing good ever lasts in our world, but only the bad."

Sorry for saying that, but it is true and might not have happened if we didn't have so many bad people in the government or have the one percent controling everything. Getting back to the story, just when someone was about to say something to this, the old giant cut in and said, "Why don't we stop talking and finish up our food so we can all go to bed and get a good night's sleep?"

We all agreed to this, and when we were done eating, the witch who had said I smelled like five ogres on hot days called my name, and when I turned to her, she said, "Before you go to bed—"

"I know!" I said before she could finish. "And I will take a bath once I know where the bathroom is."

I knew I was being rude when I said this, but the witch just said, as she nodded her head, "The first bathroom is the last door on the second floor down the left side hallways."

"Thank you," I began. "And sorry for being rude."

The witch laughed at this and then said, "That's all right, boy, I'm used to it, because nagging happens to be one of my bad habits."

"It really is since she nags me all the time," the old giant said as he left the room, but he didn't get to leave without this witch saying, "Hey, I heard that."

"Well, it's true," the old giant said.

When the giant left the kitchen, the witch turned to me and said, "There are towels for you on the right side of the bathroom doors, and we have a clean set of clothes for you in the bedroom we prepared for you, and you'll find that on the same floor and three doors before the bathroom."

And with that, I left the kitchen and soon found myself wandering around to find the first mansion bathroom available. It was a long walk, and once or twice, I needed directions to get there. Luckily, there were carved faces in some areas which told me where to go.

When I finally found this bathroom, I saw it was the size of a mall, a high school, and a large warehouse put together. It was shaped like a large square, but what amazed me about this bathroom were the toilets and the sinks, because I found out once I entered that they changed their size and shape for the person who needed them. But what really amazed me about this bathroom was the bathtub, and when I first entered, I thought I was in a pool room, but when I saw the sinks and toilets, I was shocked, because the bathtub was the size of a very large swimming pool, but deeper, which made me glad that I could swim. And just when I was about to get ready to go in, the bathtub started to rise up with water and bubble soap, and it was all coming out of nowhere, and that's when I said to myself, "Now, that's what I call magic."

After I was done with my bath and was in a new set of clothes the people of the manor gave me, I spent the rest of the time in my new room, and it was a great room and twice the size of a normal bedroom, too. It had a bed which was twice the size of a normal bed with so many blankets that were made of either cloth or fur and soft pillows as well. Stools stood on both sides of my bed with a large closet on the right side, and right in front of the bed was the door that led out into the hallway. Everything in this room was bright red, even the pillows, blankets, and bed, and the candles lighting the room were red, and I liked it.

As I was sitting on this bed and reading the map, I felt stupid about being by that boulder. As I looked out of the window behind me, I saw how dark it was starting to get, and just when I was about to put out the lights and go to sleep, my friends came into the room.

I said to them, "What's wrong, guys?"

"Oh, nothing!" Talia began.

"We just came to see you," Andria said as they all sat on the end of my bed.

"Thanks, guys!" I said.

I was glad to see them, and there were a few minutes of silence until my friend Eddy said, "So, you like your new bed?"

"I admit," I began with a laugh, "it's a lot more comfortable and warmer than the one I have at home."

"Well, we're glad to hear it," Talia said.

Another moment of silence and laughter followed this until my friend Marvin asked in an uneasy voice, "Hey, Alex, how far do we have to travel until we reach the Treasure of the Ancient Wizards?"

At that question, I picked up the map which I placed on one of the stools before they came in. After asking the map the same question, it gave me an answer, and I said, "We would be on another one of these mountains by now, meaning we still have a long way to go before we reach the treasure."

"And by that time," Eddy said, "we might have run out of food."

"And we would have starved to death," I said, "before we got to Drainton City with the amount of food we had."

"So basically, coming here was a good thing," Andria said in an 'I told you so,' voice.

I said, rolling my eyes a bit before I spoke, "Okay, I was wrong. I don't know how—"

"We're just messing with you," Talia and Andria said at the same time, which allowed me to give them a stern look when they said this, and then I said, "Still, I know I was wrong for not thinking these people wanted to help us, and the more I think about it, this is not the same situation the three travelers got themselves into."

I waited for someone to say something, but when they didn't, I went on and said, "All the same, the people here are doing us a grand favor, and we owe them a grand thanks when we are ready to leave."

"You're right, Alex!" they all said together.

"Anyway, guys," I said, trying to help the situation, "I did tell you this was not going to be easy, but that treasure is not going anywhere until we get there, which is why I don't mind how long we stay."

They all agreed to this, and after a few seconds, we all laughed a little, and then I said, "And when we finally do leave, we'll have a lot more energy than before, which will not only help us finish our journey to the treasure, but against anything we will face next."

They all gave me uneasy looks after I finished, and then my friend Andria said in a stern voice, "Are you just saying all this because you still feel guilty for spending the first night by that boulder?"

"Yes and no!" I began feeling a bit annoyed. "Because yes, I still feel guilty for what I did, but I also know a rest stop always does wonders for travelers like us."

We all fell silent after that until my friend Marvin said, "That's true, but we thought you packed enough food to last us through this adventure."

"I thought I did, too, but I also told you guys to bring some food as well since—"

"If you ask me," Talia began, looking in another direction, "I think we ate a little too much every time we stopped at a place to spend the night or had a rest. Plus, we might have eaten a lot of our food when we spent a few days in that cave, which I thought we'd be in forever."

"I think you're right, Talia!" I began. "But at least we came here where we can not only get some more food, but where we can also rest before we end this adventure."

"And to think," Marvin added, "you're the one who didn't want to come here in the first place."

We all laughed again, and after a few seconds, my friend Andria said, feeling a bit bad as she spoke, "Hey Alex, there is something else we've been meaning to ask you."

"What is it?" I said feeling a bit worried as I rose a bit from my bed when she went on and said, feeling a bit worried as she spoke, "Well, you know how none of us ever told our parents where we were going or what we were doing?"

"Yeah, I know that," I said now feeling very worried as Talia added on, "Well, what if they're looking for us right now?"

At this, I did some thinking and then said, "Well, I've been wondering the same thing since we left, and it was why I asked to leave our cell phones behind. Yes, I know I said it was probably because they might not work here, but it was—"

"We kind of had a feeling there was more to it," Eddy said, and I then said, "I didn't want to take the risk of them calling us every few seconds or trying to talk us out of this since it will benefit them as well as us in the end."

"And if you stop and think about it," Marvin said, "it was a smart option since none of us ever stop using them."

We laughed at that, and then I went on and said, "But I have hoped they are not too worried about us, because if anything happens to our families, it will be all my fault."

"Why would you think it is your fault?" Eddy said.

"Yeah," Andria put in. "We all agreed to come with you."

"But I allowed it!" I began, looking down at my blankets. "And that's why I keep saying to myself that —"

"Oh, Alex, don't say that," Talia said before I could finish, and went on in a voice that made me look at them all, "We all wanted to do this, and yes, our families are probably worried about us since we have been gone for quite some time, but it will be our own fault if something happens to them. But since they know what the five of us are like when we are together, let's hope they're not worrying too much."

I didn't want to admit she was right, and just when I was about to say something, she went on and said, "The reason we all wanted to come with you was so you can not only share this treasure with us, but because we wanted to help you. You're our best friend. We're all best friends, and we stick together no matter what. It's how it worked for us when we were in school, and it's something that will help us get to our destination."

This is a lesson you should always understand, because it's the mark of true friendships, plus having friends like this is always a good thing. That's why I was glad to have them in my life, but let's return to the story.

After Talia finished what she said, my friend Marvin then said, "She's right, Alex. Anyway, our families are going to have a hard time trying to find us since we are in another universe."

"And because we are in another universe," Andria said before I opened my mouth, "what if, by the time we get back, no time has passed?"

"I'm not so sure that will happen," I said.

"Why do you say that, Alex?" Andria said giving me an uneasy look, and what I said, hoping this would help, was, "Well, I know it's happened many times in the book series that caused me to avoid this place at first. But this is reality, and there might be a different time between this world and ours, but let's not be surprised if there isn't."

At this, they all had the kinds of faces that made me feel uneasy, which was why I now said in an uneasy voice, "But I do hope there is a different time between the two and that it is not too much time, because…"

I didn't get to finish, because at that second, the door opened and a hag popped in and said, "I don't mean to interrupt this, but it's getting late and it's time you were all in bed, so…"

None of us disobeyed, and after they all left and said their goodnights, the hag said once they were all out of earshot, "I'm so sorry, boy, but it is one of the rules here."

"Oh, don't be," I said. "Because now I can get some sleep."

The hag giggled at this, and after she shut the door, I got my wand which was on another stool and waved it, and all the lights in my room were off, and the only light came from the window as a bright moon and stars shone in. And that is what helped me sleep since I enjoy a light from the moon and stars to help me sleep.

A few hours later I started to have a dream, but this was no ordinary dream; in fact, I was not sure it was a dream at all. And the reason I say this is because I felt something I had never felt before in any of my dreams. Also, I was in a place that was nothing but a squared bluish, blackish background, and just when I was about to say something, the voice I'd been hearing many times appeared out of nowhere and said, "Welcome, m'boy, to the in-between of your dreams and your reality."

I was shocked at what I had just heard, which was why I now said in a confused and frightened voice, "Who are you, and why have I heard your voice before?"

And at my question, a man appeared out of nowhere in a strange form of bright lights which made me cover my eyes for a few seconds. All the same, this man that appeared had red, blue, and green robes, a gray beard that went down to his chest, and hair that was gray as well. He also had eyes that were brown like a tree trunk and an eight-inch-tall wizard's hat on his head which was the same colors as his robes. Again, I was completely shocked by this because this was the strangest thing that has ever happened to me, and when I was able to talk, I said, "Who are you?"

The man then said after he gave a small chuckle, "Who I am is not important, Alex. It's not always best to ask someone who they are, lad. However, the reason you have heard my voice before, my young friend, is because it was I who led you to the chest that started your adventure to find the Treasure of the Ancient Wizards."

"That was you!" I said in a surprised voice, and when I tried to say more, he said in a chuckle before he spoke, "Oh, yes, it was, boy."

I was a little surprised to hear this, which was why I now said, "But why do you want me to have this treasure, sir?"

The wizard chuckled again before saying, "Oh, I think you already know the answer to that, my friend."

"Not really, sir," I said.

The wizard then gave me a hard-to-believe look and then said, "Well, my young friend, what do you and your friends plan on doing once you get to the treasure? Meaning, what is ahead for your futures once you have this grand fortune?"

I did some thinking once he said this, and the thing I said now was, "Well, what we want to do is not only give ourselves and our families a good life, but we also want to help people."

"And how do you plan to help them?" the wizard asked.

And the answer I gave him was, "By creating more and more jobs, places to enjoy themselves, and new and easy ways to get around, even have a life without working all the time, because people need to enjoy life and not have it pass by."

At that, the wizard smiled and said, "Those were the words I wanted you to say, boy, and now I must be off, but be sure we will meet again... But next time, it won't be here."

Just before I could say something to understand more, he was gone and I awoke with a fright. It took me a while to get back to sleep, but I also believed that the dream I had might not have been a dream at all. As I lay back down, I promised myself that this was something I would not tell anyone about. I know that's wrong, but this was something too hard to believe even if I did tell them.

The next few weeks were the best my friends and I could ever remember having, and what we got to do was not only have as much fun as we wanted, but also feast every three hours and hear many great stories of the Magicalworld. These stories were mostly told by the old giant and Comdust the centaur, but sometimes by someone else. We also got to sleep as long as we liked, even all day if we wanted. But the best thing we got to do was go hunting with the hunting party, and on the fifth trip with them, which was in the valley the old giant pointed out to me when I spent the first day and a half by that boulder. Nevertheless, I was glad to be in this valley because looking at the map, there was no way my friends and I were going to pass by this place when we were ready to leave the manor.

On this trip here I was able to catch and kill three unicorns and bring down two dragons, even lure a few giant spiders into a trap. Even my friend Eddy was able to conquer his fears of giant snakes. When he and a few others hunted and caught a sea serpent that was bigger than the one we had encountered before, at first we all felt a bit guilty about hunting animals in another dimension, but we discovered that no matter how many were hunted, there were still many other animals, and the number one rule about hunting in this world is, "Only hunt animals that have a huge amount of herds or packs, meaning only hunt those in strong numbers.

Never hunt those that are at risk of being wiped out, because that is not a hunter but a…"

I really didn't want to put the word in, but all the same, when I was able to catch and kill a very large dragon, the brown bushy-bearded wizard said, "Well done, boy, and since you're the one who caught it, you can have your favorite part to eat tonight."

It really was the greatest moment, and not just on this trip, but on many trips we had with the hunting party. Even my friends enjoyed the kills they made on these trips, and we continued to join them on these hunts, but not so much Andria. That is because she was a great animal lover, and what one of the hunters said to her was, "We hunt to eat; we don't hunt for pleasure, gain, or trophies."

"Even animals hunt other animals for food," another hunter said to her. This still didn't help, which was why she stopped coming on these trips. As time went by, we were soon a great help around the manor as many of them asked us to help out from time to time, which we were happy to do, but at least we didn't have to do it alone, just help many with their routine jobs every chance we got or if they asked.

One morning, when I was having a strange but good dream, I was woken up by Wendy, and before I could say anything, she said, "I need your help in the garden."

"Okay!" I said with a yawn. "Just—"

"Drink this!" she said before I could finish, and then she gave me a bottle full of strange-looking potion.

After I drank the whole bottle, I got dressed and followed Wendy to the garden. I'd been out here a few times since my friends and I had come here, and not only was this the biggest garden you could ever hope to see, but it was also one of the largest areas on the grounds with many areas of fruits and vegetables, most growing from the ground and others growing from small, strange-looking trees. There were also large cornfields on one side and a large pumpkin patch in another area, and many different plants, flowers, and small streams of water in many other areas, and when the sun rises, this area gets a lot of sunshine.

As Wendy and I got a wheelbarrow, she said as we walked to the heart of this garden, "You have your wand on you, right?"

I took it out and showed her.

"Good, and sorry I woke you, but I needed an extra hand, and since you can do magic—" she murmured.

"I understand," I began before she could finish. "But what do you want me to do first?"

She smiled and then said, "Well, first we need more wheelbarrows before we can start."

It took a while, but after a few minutes, we had about ten or twelve of them, and that's when she said, "Ready?"

When I said "Yes", both of us cast a spell at the same time, and at this spell, so many fruits, vegetables, and plants came shooting out of the ground and into many of the wheelbarrows, which only took fifteen minutes to do. When this was done, Wendy sent the wheelbarrows back to the manor's main building and then caused two drinks to appear for the both of us and chairs for us to sit on.

As we sat, she said as she took a sip from her drink, "Normally, I do this by myself, because the gardens are my domain, but I needed this all done before sunrise."

"And spells work faster!" I said after taking a sip from my own drink. "When they're cast by more than one person."

She laughed at this and then said, "That is true, and you and your friends have become a big help since you've been here."

"It's the least we can do," I said with a smile, and it allowed Wendy to say, "Hey, you and your friends are not just a big help to us; you've become members of the family." A moment of silence fell after this, and when Wendy looked up into the sky, she then said, "It's almost time for breakfast, so we'd better head back in."

More time had now passed since we'd been here, and one morning, I was sitting in between an elf with a squeaky voice and the old giant. Something was on my mind, and even a great breakfast could not get it out of my head, so I said to the elf while hoping I was choosing my words right, "I don't mean to ask this, but how long will it take until we are ready to leave once again?"

At this question, the elf said, "We'll have enough food and all your clothes plus new ones ready in a few more days."

I was just about to say "Thank you" when the old giant said, "Why are you asking anyway, Alex?"

I knew this was coming, and the answer I gave him was, "A few days ago, I almost forgot the real reason my friends and I are here, and don't get me wrong—"

"Oh, I understand," the old giant said with a laugh. "And you just want to reach the treasure and go home, right?" I was about to say something to this giant, but he went on and said, "Don't worry about it. Even though you and your friends have been great company and have now become part of this family, we don't want to keep you from what you're really here for."

A moment of silence passed, and just when I was about to say something, he then said, "By the way, if you and your friends would like to spend the day down in the basement library like you planned to do, you can."

After breakfast, I met up with my friends, and we went down many flights of stairs just to get to this library. This was the biggest library you could ever hope to see or imagine, plus being down here was like being in the bottom center of the mountain, which it was in. But getting back to the story, this library had thousands and thousands of shelves covered with books, and like the stuff in the bathroom, it could change its size and shape for the person who wanted it.

Some of these books, like the ones I had, could read themselves, and a few would remain blank until you read the first sentence. I wish I could tell you the names of all these titles, but that will take a very long time to do. But this was a good place to come, not just for my friends, but for myself since I do enjoy reading and reading can be more fun than television.

Another week followed, and now we were on our last day here, and everyone in the manor made us a grand and wonderful goodbye feast and made sure everything was just right, and that's when I got up and said, "Thank you for everything you've done for us."

"We're very grateful for all of it," Marvin added.

"It's nothing," a female giant said. "But we do wish you could stay and live with us."

At the words of this young witch, we began saying things like,

"So do we!"

"But we didn't just come to this world to have the wonderful time that you gave us."

"And we are a bit homesick and miss our families!"

"But we will come back one day."

"That's a promise."

Every one of them smiled, and what the female giant said again was, "We know we can't force you to stay."

"And we do hope you reach your destination safely and alive," the old giant added on, and then one of the witches said, "And because we know you don't have that much to go when you reach Drainton City, some of us are going to fly you down the mountain tomorrow." I wanted to say something to this, but this witch went on and said, "The way from here to Drainton City, if you take the routes on that map, will lead you into messes we do not want to see the five of you get into. We would offer to fly you the rest of the way, but we might get stopped in midair, and that will put you all in danger."

When I asked why, the old giant said, "What the five of you must do when you get to Drainton City is not, I repeat, not tell anyone there that you're humans."

"Why? What happens if we do?" I said with a worried voice, and what another witch said to this was, "They'll capture you and do a lot of horrible experiments on you, even kill the five of you, something we do not want."

"Well, thank you for telling us this," Talia began, feeling a bit scared. "But how do we pass without being detected?"

This made a few of the hags smile and allowed one to say, "We have that taken care of."

"How?" Andria asked.

The hag went on and said, "We packed a few witch and wizard robes in your rucksacks so you can blend in with everyone in the city."

"And!" The young witch said, "All your stuff will be at the door tomorrow when we are ready to fly you down the mountain."

We were grateful for this, but it still made me say, feeling a bit worried as I spoke, "So what time will we be leaving?"

"Right after lunch!" the witch said. "That way you can get there before dark and then walk through it the next day, because it will take you all day just to pass through that city."

"And a good place for you to spend the night," the old giant began, "is a small forest right before the city, and you don't have to worry about being caught while walking into the city."

"Because!" Comdust added, "None of the witches and wizards in that city ever leave unless they are on a broomstick, and we do wish you the best of luck and hope one day we will all meet again."

Hours had now passed and everyone was asleep—everyone but me, that is. I was having a hard time sleeping that night because I had a lot on my mind, and no matter how hard I tried, I could not get to sleep. After another few minutes had passed, I decided to give up, and doing that caused the candles in my room to light up.

At first, I thought of just staying in my room reading the map, but I realized that was one of the things that was on my mind and stopping me from sleeping. And so, after getting off my bed and putting on a silver-striped bathrobe given to me by the people of the manor, I opened my door and began to wander around.

I soon found myself in the basement library and got a few books I never got a chance to read. As I entered, a light magically came on as I began looking for the books I wanted. After I found them, I thought of just reading here, but then I thought of going to another part of the mansion.

The place I was in now was a living room, but like almost everything in this manor, it was twice the size of a normal living room and, like the kitchen and the bathroom, had couches and chairs that could change their size and shape for the person who wanted it. I noticed this when a chair by the fireplace changed to just the right way for me to sit in it, and speaking of the fireplace, it was the biggest thing in the room, and as I sat in the chair, the fire magically started, and all the lights in the living room came on. I also saw a ruby-colored carpet that covered the whole floor, and all the walls and ceilings were silver. As I was reading, I soon noticed this was what I needed even though I was alone in this room.

I wasn't alone for long, because as I turned a page of the book I was reading, a voice from behind me said my name. I jumped and turned to see that it was Comdust, and just when I was about to say something, he said as he kneeled his horse half to sit, "What are you doing up at this hour?"

"I couldn't sleep and had a lot on my mind," I said.

Comdust laughed at this and then said, "That's usually the best excuse for being up at this time, but I bet you also have some worries on your mind as well."

At this, I closed the book and put it on a stool that appeared out of nowhere along with the other books I had and said, "Well, you know how my friends and I are leaving tomorrow?"

From the look on Comdust's face, this seemed like a subject he did not want to talk about, which was why he said in a sad voice, "I do, and we will miss the five of you, because you've become a great part of our lives, but you came here for the treasure, a treasure all of us here are happy to know will finally be put to good use."

"Well!" I began as a tear came into my eye. "I'm just starting to have second thoughts about leaving this place."

"Why?" Comdust asked.

"Yes, boy, why?"

Both Comdust and I jumped at the sound of this new voice and soon saw that it was the old giant who had just come in the room. I wanted to say something to him, but he then said laying on a couch that had just changed to the right size for him, "I see I am not the only one having trouble sleeping tonight. All the same, Alex, how come you're starting to have second thoughts of completing your quest?"

I didn't answer right away, but when I did, the thing I said was, "These past few weeks have been the best I ever had in my life and—"

"And it's just going to be hard to be back to how it was when this all started," the old giant said just when I was about to say something.

Comdust said, "Well, my young friend, we understand that it will be hard for you and your friends to be out there on your own again. That's why a few witches and wizards wanted to fly you down the mountain tomorrow afternoon."

"All the same!" the old giant said who went on by saying, "We may have plenty of space for you and your friends, but don't you want to return to your families?"

This was another thing I almost forgot about, which leads me to say this: Sometimes when you're enjoying a good life or a very great visit, you forget a few things, things you never want to forget, and when I said this had slipped my mind, Comdust then said, "Well, that is something you can blame me for since I am the one who found you and your friends and brought you here, but if I remember, you weren't—"

"And I still feel guilty about that," I said before he could finish. "And it's another reason I'm having second thoughts about leaving."

"We understand," the old giant began. "But like you once said, someone wants you to have this treasure. But I do believe one day we will meet again."

This was the very thing that really helped me and made me yawn, which was why Comdust then said, "Head back to bed, boy, and don't worry about your books; we'll take them back for you."

And so, after saying my goodnights and "Thank you," I made my way back to bed.

5

The Sisters in the City

The next day — after having a really great feast and some time to say our goodbyes to everyone in the Magical Mountain Manor — we were now flying down the mountain on broomsticks holding tightly to the one who was flying it. I was not so keen on this at first since I have a fear of heights, but luckily, it was not that bad of a ride. Also, we didn't get to leave the manor until late in the afternoon, but when we did leave, we met by the boulder I had spent the first night at. However, when we came to the bottom of the mountain and on the White Brick Path again, the wizards and witches told us once again what we had to do so we do not get caught by anyone in the city. And after we said we understood, one of them then said, "Good, and again, we would have flown you the rest of the way to where you're going, but we couldn't risk getting stopped in midair." Again, we said we understood, and after they said goodbye, they flew back up the mountain and out of sight.

When they were gone, I got out the map and we walked in the direction of Drainton City. We also took our time because we were not going to spend the night in the city since there was not that much cover. And since our rucksacks were heavier than before this all began, it was the best we could do. Also, we didn't care how heavy our rucksacks were now due to the fact most of the things in them were gifts from our new friends, friends that none of us wanted to leave.

When we reached the border of the city and were walking through a forest on the path we saw it was getting dark, so after we came off the path, we started to look for a clear area to spend the night. When at last we found a great spot to set up camp, I performed a few spells to ensure we were protected and then made a fire. As the fire began to burn and settle, I took out some of the food and began to cook a hot dinner.

When it was done and we all began eating, my friend Talia said as she swallowed her food, "So Alex, what is the plan for tomorrow?"

It took me a while to answer because I was eating, too, and when I was done, I said, "The plan is, we just get through Drainton City without any problems or trouble with any of the citizens."

"That's it?" Marvin asked.

"Well, I'm hoping more will come to me in my sleep, but what I'm really hoping even more is that none of you get caught in the city." I answered, chewing thoughtfully after.

"Why would you think we'll get caught and not you?" Andria put in.

"Because!" I said feeling annoyed. "I'm the only one here that has a wand and knows how to do magic, so I have a better chance of pulling this off than you guys." This brought a lot of uneasy looks on their faces, which was why I now said, hoping this might help, "But I do hope we pull this off and get through that city without any trouble from anyone who lives there."

"So do we!" they all said together.

After a few seconds, my friend Marvin said, "Anyway, the odds are on our side, because like we were told back at the Magical Mountain Manor, no one in this world believes creatures like us exist. So as long as we keep our mouths shut and don't draw any attention to ourselves, we have nothing to worry about."

"You make a good point, Marvin," I said feeling a bit uneasy, and then I stood up and went on by saying, "But right now, let's forget about this and go and get some sleep, because we are going to need it. Plus, if we get up at a good time, we can get through the city before the day ends."

The next morning, we all woke up before the sun rose and went over the plan for a few minutes. After it was clear on what we had to do, we all got into our witch and wizard robes. Then I cast a spell to pack everything up, and then we left this area and headed toward the city. When we entered Drainton City, we looked around and saw that the city was like looking at both Boston and New York at once and that the place was completely normal, and after so much we'd seen so far in this world, this was the last thing we expected. Then I remembered an old saying which I quoted as we walked on: "Things are not always as they seem."

As we walked through the city we saw that a lot of the witches and wizards living here were not very friendly. None of them were like any of the witches and wizards we had met at the Magical Mountain Manor. That's why we were grateful we were able to blend in and just walk past, because we were not in the mood for trouble. However, when we reached the heart of the city, we decided to stop for a while and have a bite to eat.

Luckily, where we stopped, we saw a few stone-made picnic tables, and since there was no one around this area, we all sat, ate, and rested. However, halfway through a good bite to eat and a few good drinks, I started to hear something. It was strange, too, because I noticed I was the only one who could hear it since no one else was bothered. Nevertheless, the thing I was hearing was someone crying, and it was a girl, too, which began to worry me.

Just as I got up and began to walk away, my friend Marvin said, "Alex, where are you going?"

This did cause me to stop and say, "I'm going to find out where that sound is coming from."

None of them liked what I had just said, as they were not that keen on me doing this. However, just as I was about to take another step, my friend Talia said in a worried voice, "Are you sure that is a good idea?"

"I'll be fine," I said turning back to them. "Just wait here until I get back."

It took me a while to find where the crying was coming from, and when at last I found the source, it was down a dark, narrow, crooked alleyway. What I was seeing now was a girl, but to me, I thought I was looking at the most beautiful girl that ever existed. When I walked up to her, I said, hoping this would help and hoping she would not be afraid, "Hello!"

She looked up at me in surprise as I went on and said, "I noticed you were sad, and I wanted to see if there is anything I can do to help you."

When she looked into my face, I started to feel goosebumps and a few other things as well. Also, what she looked like was this: She had long, black lighted hair and eyes that were bright green. She even had skin that looked soft as a pillow and wore bright blue witch's robes, and when she spoke, it was, in my opinion, the most beautiful voice I had ever heard in my life, even if it was sad at first, which was also starting to make me sad as she said, wiping a few tears off her face, "No one can help me. Just leave me alone."

"But why are you crying?" I asked as I sat by her and put an arm around her shoulder.

I don't know what made me do that, but it seemed to calm her down as she now said, "I'm crying because no one likes me."

This made me almost cry, so I said, "But why wouldn't anyone like someone like you?"

I didn't feel like this was helping, and just when I was about to say something that might help, she leaned on me and said as she cried onto my wizard's robe, which caused me to pat her on the back, "No one likes me because I can't do magic of any kind. I can't do spells, enchantments, hexes, or even shoot a spark of any kind out of a wand. And a lot of people call me names like 'freak', 'you-not-a-witch', and a bunch of other names I don't want to say. They even say that I don't belong anywhere and that I don't deserve to exist."

"That's cruel!" I said as I began to stroke her hair, and then I said as she got up and looked the other way, "By the way, what is your name?"

The second I said this, she turned to face me and said as she wiped a few tears from her face, "Cordelia!"

"Well, Cordelia!" I said trying my best not to smile. "I know how you feel; where my friends and I come from, we get picked on all the time because we are not the same as they are, and most of the time, we fight back to defend ourselves. Unfortunately, it always gets us into trouble because the people in charge always take the side of the ones who start the fight instead of those who are just trying to defend themselves."

This seemed to cheer her up, and when I explained how much trouble I was always in because of the bad teachers I had before the teacher I had in the beginning of the story, she then said feeling a bit unease, "But what if they use wands on you?"

At that I whispered into her ear and said, "Where we come from, no one can do magic."

"They can't?" she said as she took a step back, and she started to look into my eyes, which almost made me faint, but then I said, "Yeah, my friends and I come from a world where no one can do or even believes in magic."

"I thought worlds like that were just myths," she said.

"Well, they're not," I said as we both giggled, and then I said, "I mean, I was given magic just to get my friends and myself here, but that's not the point; the point here is, do you have family to go to? Meaning, do you have any parents, siblings, or relatives to go to when you feel no one understands?"

This made her upset again and say, "My family doesn't even love me; they think I'm nothing but a waste of space and an embarrassment to them all."

I felt very disgusted when she said this, and that's when I said in a very angry voice, almost shouting as I spoke, "Now, that's just wrong in so many ways."

"I know it is," she said feeling a bit angry herself. "But that's my life and I have to accept it."

"Not anymore, you don't," I said without thinking, but it caused her to look at me with a shocked face and say, "What did you say?"

It took a while for me to speak because I wasn't sure I was doing the right thing, but then I realized I was when I saw a smile on Cordelia's face, which I liked seeing, and that's why I now said, "Talking to you, Cordelia, has got me thinking, and I think you should come with me and my friends on our adventure. Leave this life of yours forever, and we will give you a new and better life where we come from."

"You'll do that for me?" she said looking half-happy and half-surprised.

"Of course!" I said with a smile. "No one deserves to have a miserable life, not even someone like you."

The last words of this sentence are words I wished I had never said, but before I go on, let me just say something for future reference. Me giving this offer to this non-witch is different than a stranger coming up and doing it to you, because this is how a lot of kidnapping happens, and even though it's not the case here, you should still never accept an offer from someone you don't know, because it may not end the same way it's happening here. Plus, to treat others badly because they are different is wrong, because everyone is different in ways we do not understand, something barely anyone understands to this day, which is why many feel alone in this world. So if you know someone in a case like this, help them and show them they are not alone.

But getting back to the story, after Cordelia said "Yes," to my offer, we both walked back to the others. I told her my name and the names of my friends and the reason we came to this world.

That made her say in a voice only I could hear, since we were walking through a crowd of witches and wizards who were starting to give us suspicious looks, "You're serious you and your friends are really going after the Treasure of the Ancient Wizards?"

"Yes!" I said as she took my hand and I accepted. "And we're almost there, and when at last we get there and get as much as we can get, we'll get to go home and you can have a new and better life."

"I'm really looking forward to that, Alex." She looked at me as she said this and gave me a smile that really made me weak in the knees. However, the second she said this, everything around me stopped; even she stopped, but still smiled as she did. Nevertheless, I was worried until I heard the sound of clapping coming from nowhere, and a second later, the wizard, the same wizard who had appeared to me in my dream back at the Magical Mountain Manor, appeared again and said, "Well done, Alex, well done."

"What are you talking about?" I said feeling confused, which made him say as he stopped clapping, "You've completed your final task, my boy, that has given you every right to have the Treasure of the Ancient Wizards."

"What do you mean, sir?" I said still feeling confused, but he just said, with a small chuckle in his voice, "What I mean, Alex, is that I was hoping you would hear Cordelia crying, find her, and ask her to join you on the rest of your journey to the Treasure of the Ancient Wizards, and you did. Now your path to the treasure is clear, so I say goodbye again until we meet again."

And after he was gone, everything was back to normal, which allowed me and Cordelia to walk back and find my friends. When at last we got back to the others, they did not like the fact I brought back someone. They also didn't like the fact I wanted her to come with us, which caused her to almost leave and me to say in anger, "Guys, I am not leaving her; she has a sad and lonely life in this city just because she can't do magic. And we of all people know what it is like to be treated badly just because we are all different. So if she does not come with us, the adventure ends right here, and we risk getting caught."

None of them were pleased about what I had just said, but I was not going to leave Cordelia here, not just because of what the wizard had just said, but because I believed she deserved a better life than this. However, after a few seconds, they all said she could come, and all six of us pressed on once again. After we got out of the city, they were glad that she came with us since she helped us get out of here faster. It turned out she knew a lot of shortcuts and good areas to go past that no one enjoys passing. When we thought we were being followed, she helped us lose them; even I was able to give a false trail. The reason we thought we were almost followed was because of my outburst, and that might have caused a few citizens to come after us. But because of Cordelia's help, we didn't have to deal with them.

As we traveled, we saw that it was starting to get dark. And as it did, we came to a soft stone hill with a grassy area on the top and a good cover to protect us. This place was even as far from the city as we wanted, meaning it was a good and safe place to spend the night. After we set up camp and had a fire burning nicely and easily, I began to cook some food. As I was cooking, I took out the map, and what it said now was,

Congratulations! You and your friends are almost to the Treasure of the Ancient Wizards. But you still have two more challenges to deal with before you come to the end of this adventure. One is the Lava Ponds where you have to be very careful or you'll fall into the lava and die, and the second is the Haunted Dark Forest. It is in that forest you'll face your worst fears, your darkest nightmares, and the dark spirits that live in that forest. But once you make it

143

past, you are at the spot where the Treasure of the Ancient Wizards is kept. Once you reach the treasure, your adventure will come to an end, and I hope you've enjoyed every second of it.

After I was done reading this through a few times, I put the map back in my pocket and started to see if the food I was cooking, which was dragon and unicorn meat, was ready and saw it still had a long way to go since this kind of food takes a while to cook. This allowed me to look in another direction, and I saw Cordelia looking sad as she stared in the direction of the city.

I had a feeling she was still upset, so when I called her over and asked if she was okay, she said as she sat by my side, "I'm just worried that I'm putting you and your friends in—"

"I don't think you are," I said knowing what was at the end of this sentence, which I thought would help, but she tried to say something which caused me to say before she got the words out, "If someone was looking for you, we would have company by now, company that my friends and I can take care of. Just don't worry so much, Cordelia, because you're safe with us, we promise you. I promise you."

This put a smile on Cordelia's face, which was making me smile even when she said, "You really think I'm doing the right thing by running away with you and your friends?"

"Of course I do!" I said smiling as I spoke. "No one, not even a beautiful girl like you, deserves to have the life you just ran away from."

She giggled and blushed at this and continued to blush as she said, "You're very sweet, Alex, you know that?"

And what I said, smiling back, in a very nervous voice because she was making me feel things I don't think I could ever feel if I never met her, was, "Not really."

"Well, I think you are," she said as she wrapped her arms around mine, and she went on as she put her head toward mine, "Plus, you are the first boy who has ever been kind to me; in fact, you're the only person who has ever been kind to me."

I felt embarrassed as she said this, but it didn't stop me from saying, feeling a bit stupid as I spoke, "And you're the only girl who has ever…"

I stopped because I didn't have the courage to finish what I wanted to say, something I never had a problem with until I met her, but Cordelia just kissed me on the cheek and said, taking a few steps back and in a voice that was making me nervous, "You don't have to say what you're trying to say, but I am grateful for what you did for me today." We both fell silent for a second, and then she said, "Do you want my help cooking this food?"

"Yes, I could use some help," I said. And to that, we just enjoyed each other's company, but as we did, my friends were watching everything that was happening. They were all on the other side of the tent watching all this happening and saying things like,

"Alex has a girlfriend!"

"Oh, isn't that romantic?"

"Don't they make a great couple?"

"Isn't that sweet?"

I was glad I didn't hear any of this, because if I did, I would not be happy. But right now, nothing made me happier than being there with Cordelia, because it was the greatest moment of my life, a moment I never wanted to end nor for her to leave my sight, because I felt my happiness would end if she did. However, when the food was ready, we called the others to come and get it, and all six of us enjoyed a grand dinner. One thing I noticed when we started to eat was that all my friends were laughing, and when I asked what was so funny, they all said at different times, "Nothing."

The looks on their faces made me wonder if they were telling me the truth, but then I thought maybe this was something I didn't want to know. After we were done eating and I put out the fire, we all went into the tent and I started to wonder where Cordelia was going to sleep, because I only packed for five, not six, and when Cordelia saw that all of us were thinking this, she then said, "You guys don't have to worry about me, because I already have my own bed and sleeping bag. Actually, I have all my stuff with me since I have it with me at all times."

"You take your stuff with you wherever you go?" Andria asked, and what Cordelia said now was, "Only because a lot of people like to steal my stuff."

"Well, you don't have to worry about that with us; in fact, you never have to be unhappy again when this is all over," At that, I hoped something would happen, but when it didn't, I then said, "But right now, let's all get some sleep, because we have another long day tomorrow."

And so, after we all found spots in the tent, all six of us fell asleep at once, and as we slept, I noticed that Cordelia's hand was in mine, and this was the very thing that helped me sleep.

No sooner did we all fall asleep and a few hours passed Cordelia heard something, and I heard it, too. This thing we were hearing was someone calling her name, and so, trying her best not to wake us all up, she kissed me on the check and left.

It didn't take her long to find the source, because no sooner was she a mile away from the tent, then she came face-to-face with a witch. This witch was wearing a long, light witch's robe and had a sour face along with dark blonde hair and eyes, the same as Cordelia's, and the first thing she said to this witch was, "Rain, what are you doing here?"

This witch felt a bit worried when she said this, which was why she now said in an understanding voice, "Looking for you."

"Why?" Cordelia said in anger, which caused silence to fall between these two.

Finally, the witch called Rain coaxed in a stern and worried voice, trying her best not to start something bad, "Cordelia, I know you had a bad day, but—"

"A bad day!" Cordelia said in anger. "I've had a bad life and I'm done with it."

Rain looked a bit upset, but it didn't stop her from saying, "Cordelia, where will you go? You have—"

"I've been given an offer," she said as her temper began to rise. "And I'm taking it!"

Rain was not happy to hear this. But she was the kind of person who doesn't give up so easily, so she came up to Cordelia and said, trying to drag her away, "Enough! I'm taking you home."

"I'm not going home with you," Cordelia said with so much anger Rain fell to the ground. She went on, "I've had enough of what my life is like and enough of you always being the one Mom and Dad love the most."

Rain felt hurt at this, and before I go on, I have something I want to say which will help you understand this situation. In some families, there is sometimes a black sheep, meaning there is someone who doesn't fit in no matter what they do. Some feel bad and try to do something about it, and there are those who become something they should have never become in the first place, which is why I say that fitting in is not always a good thing; it's best to be yourself and never care what anyone else thinks, because as long as you are yourself and never care what anyone else thinks, you are on the path to a grand future. I might have said something like this in another book, but like I said a few pages ago, it helps situations like this and sometimes you need to repeat yourself even if no one wants to hear it.

Another thing to say before I take you back into the story is that in some families that have a black sheep and what some call the perfect child—something that's very wrong because, in my opinion, there is no such thing as perfect—there are situations in which the so-called perfect child will laugh in the glory they have, meaning they only care about themselves and don't care how their black sheep sibling or anyone else around them is treated. This is wrong, because everyone should be treated as equals; if not, then it will turn back on you in a way you will not like.

The point I am really trying to make here is that if a parent shows more love to one child and treats any others like dirt, they might become something you might not like, but on most occasions, they succeed in grand and wonderful ways. And that might cause them to not want you in their lives anymore or anyone from their past. But, getting back to this situation, on rare occasions like this one here, where the perfect child tries to help their black sheep sibling, it's not always the way they want. And I say this because even though the black sheep of the family knows they do not fit in, the perfect child will try to see that they do. Sometimes it's because they are afraid they will make it on their own, which is wrong, because everyone deserves a chance to prove themselves and to show that they can take care of themselves because the people who take care of you will not be around forever. But... that doesn't mean you should deny help when it is offered.

But enough of my lessons; let's get back to the story and where I left off. What Cordelia was saying to Rain now was, "All my life, Mom and Dad treated me like I was nothing because of my lack of performing magic, while you, sister, got everything you always wanted and I've put up with it for far too long. That's why enough is enough and I'm leaving for good and never coming back."

Rain looked like she was about to cry, and the thing she said now was, "So where are you going?"

"I'm not telling you that, sister, but I am hoping where I'm going is better than what I'm leaving behind."

Rain wanted to turn around, but then she said in a surprised voice, "You're with the travelers, aren't you?"

Cordelia was shocked to hear her sister say this, so she said, hoping this would help this situation, "What travelers?"

"The travelers who are after the Treasure of the Ancient Wizards," she said in an uneasy voice. "The very treasure the people of Drainton City have been protecting for many years."

"But how do you even know about them?" Cordelia asked with a bit of anger in her voice.

Rain calmly replied, hoping to end the fight, "My friend was on vacation on the other side of the Great Mountains, and when they were enjoying a swim in the Long Wide Lake, the body of a sea serpent came at them, making them all sick. Also, the Rob Gang met them and spread the word after they were outsmarted, something no one has ever done before. And after a few from the villages in the mountains noticed that there were five strangers who had a map and were keeping to the White Brick Path, many made the connection, so..."

"So if you do anything to them..." Cordelia started, but Rain cut through and gritted her teeth, "You'll what?"

Although Rain was shocked that Cordelia was standing up to her, she was ready for a fight. And just when she was about to say something, we appeared and I said, which really shocked Rain, "If you try anything, you'll have us to deal with."

Rain looked at each and every one of us, and the thing she said now, trying her best not to be afraid, was, "So you're the travelers. I can't believe I am meeting you."

"Well, we don't want to fight you," Talia said.

"But we do want to talk," I said, and I went on by saying, "So please follow us."

And so she did, and as we were walking back to our camp, Cordelia whispered into my ear, "Are you sure this is a good idea?"

"She's right," Andria began. "If she goes back and —"

"I understand your concerns, guys," I said before anyone could say another word. "But I have a feeling if we talk to her, she might let us press on without alerting the city, and hearing that the people of Drainton City know about us I'd like to know if there is more to it." The second I said this, we were back at our camp, and after I made another fire, we offered Rain a place to sit. And the first thing I said after passing around something to eat for everyone was, "I was the one who asked Cordelia to come with us."

After she took a bite from her food, she then said, "So basically, you're kidnapping my sister."

"She could have said no!" Andria said with some attitude.

"And I didn't," Cordelia began, "because there is nothing for me here."

Silence fell after that, and after I passed around something for all of us to drink, I then said to Rain, "So please tell us, how did the people of Drainton City find out about us? No one has found out about us the whole time we've been here and—"

"I'll tell you that!" Rain said after taking a gulp from her drink. "When you tell me why you want the Treasure of the Ancient Wizards."

I looked at the others and then said, "Very well!" And so I told her almost everything, but I left out the voice and the wizard because that was not something I told my friends, and I couldn't tell her. But I did mention the chest and how I got magic and had to understand everything about this world.

After I got to the end of this, Rain gave me a look that said she didn't believe me, which was why Eddy said, knowing this might help, "Hey, none of us knew about this treasure until now."

"But moving on," I said giving Eddy a look that said to be quiet, and after I finished my drink, I then said, "Now that we've told you why we came for this treasure, please tell us how the people of Drainton City found out about us."

Rain was hoping to get out of this, but a deal is a deal, and the thing she said, feeling a bit uneasy as she spoke, was, "Well, like I said to my sister here, when my friend who was on vacation near the Long Wide Lake said she saw a dead sea serpent floating toward them and the marks showing that it was in a huge fight, she was worried, and when you were traveling in the mountains, word got to the city. And since you kept to the path, many were able to make the connection and knew you had to pass the city to get to the treasure, so they planned an ambush for you."

"Which didn't work," Eddy said as we all laughed at this since we never saw any sign of a trap when we were in the city, which allowed Rain to now say, "Unfortunately, you made friends with the people of the Magical Mountain Manor."

"What do they have to do with this?" I said with a bit of anger, but Rain went on and said, "When the witches and wizards of that place discovered we were waiting to capture you, they threatened many people in the city and said if we laid a hand or a spell on any of you, they'd harm us, and so many fear their wrath more than anything else in this world."

"Well, that explains why they wanted us to be careful," Marvin whispered to Talia, and what I said to Rain now was, "They never showed any sign that they can do anything—"

"Well, when it comes to people they really care about," Rain said before I could finish, then finished by saying, "they will do anything to ensure no one will come an inch near them, plus no one was able to track you once you were at that manor." Now we understood why they kept us there for so long and why they gave us what we needed to pass the city.

Nevertheless, just when one of us was about to say something else to our guest, she then said, "What I'd like to know now is, why are you taking my sister away?"

I really thought she got the point, but she didn't, so I said, "Because no one deserves the life she was having, and if you love your sister, you'll let her choose her own way."

"And I choose to go with them," Cordelia said finishing this all up.

Rain was sad when she said this, but it made her finally see that she did not know what was best for her sister. So she said, looking down as she spoke and feeling like a very bad person as she now said "All right, take her if she's not going to be happy here with her family or in Drainton City. Maybe she'll be happy when she finally finds what she is looking for. All I ask is that you take care of her and do what I failed to do."

"You have my word," I said, then going on and saying, "And would you like to spend the night here with us since—?"

"Oh, no, thank you," Rain said as she got up. "I can find my way back in the dark, but I advise you to be careful on the rest of your journey. I will not turn you in, but you might bump into others who will."

"And if we do," I said after she finished, "we'll be ready for them."

"We are not the kind of people you want to mess with," Talia said giggling as she said this.

Rain laughed and then said, "That might be something I'll let slip if anyone tries to come after you."

As she was about to leave, Cordelia got up and said, "You want me to walk you down the hill?"

When Rain said "Yes," both sisters walked away and I was worried, but I had a feeling she'd be back. Nevertheless, when they both got to the bottom of the hill, Rain turned to her sister and said, "Is there another reason why you are going with them?"

"Why do you ask?" Cordelia said feeling a bit embarrassed, but Rain went on and said, "Well, I couldn't help but notice the way you were looking at the one called Alex."

Cordelia did not answer but began to blush, which made Rain say with a laugh in her voice, "You like him, don't you?"

This caused Cordelia to say in a fast and nervous voice, "I don't know what you—"

"Oh, come on, Cordelia," Rain said before she could finish, going on by saying in a smiling voice, "You know I have a gift for things like this, so…"

And to that, Cordelia turned away from her sister and said, feeling very embarrassed as she spoke, "I know I just met Alex, but ever since he found me in that alley and got me to be happy, I felt something I've never felt before, something I don't think I can ever feel if he never came to my aid and asked me to come with him and his friends."

I know I am the one telling the story and I know I was not present for this, and how I found out about this is something I cannot tell you. But the thing I will tell you is that things like this happen from time to time. It is called love at first sight, the very thing you never see a lot of these days, but it doesn't mean it can't still happen, even if it is in a story like this. But getting back, the second Cordelia said what she said, Rain smiled and said, "Well, he seems okay for you, but I wish I could get to know more about the one called Talia."

"What do you mean?" Cordelia said as she turned back to face her sister.

"I mean," she said feeling embarrassed and blushing a bit as she spoke, "I thought she was, was…"

She couldn't speak, but Cordelia understood what she was saying, which was why she now said with a laugh, "Well, why don't you come with us and—?"

"I can't do that!" She said feeling a bit bad, "Someone has to make sure you guys get to your destination without any trouble, and someone needs…"

She wanted to say more, but Cordelia understood, and just when she wanted to say something, Rain just said, "Well, goodbye, sister, and enjoy a new life with your boyfriend."

"He's not my boyfriend!" Cordelia said quickly at a high tone.

Rain just laughed and said, "All the same, talking to these travelers, especially that Talia…" She smiled and blushed when she said her name, then went on and said, hoping this would help, "I know you're in good hands, so I'll go, and wherever you go, I hope there is a chance I might get to visit or meet you again."

And with that, she disappeared, and Cordelia stood there for a few seconds watching before coming back. We were all waiting for her to come back, and the thing we asked her on her return was if her sister was always like that. She then told us that for most of their lives, she had tried to help her, but it was not the help she needed. "I know she means well," she said finishing this all up. "But she was the one my parents loved the most, and I was nothing to them. They even forgot my name from time to time."

"Which we are sorry for," I began, going on by saying, "But why was she so desperate in keeping you home?"

It took a while for Cordelia to answer because she didn't know what to say; however, the thing she said now was, "Because she believed that it's where I belonged even though she knew I could never fit in no matter how hard I tried."

"Sounds like she was trying to hold you back," Eddy said.

"In some ways, she was," Cordelia began. "But she believed she knew what was best."

Again, that is never right, because you should never hold someone back, especially if they're meant to do great things. Because everyone has a different path in their lives, and as long as they never cause trouble, they should follow it. But never try to decide the path for someone else to take, because that can do more harm than good.

But getting back to the story, after Cordelia told us that Rain was upset about her coming with us, she was still willing to let her go, and knowing all this made me think about my own sister. And when I told them all what my sister could be like and that I was never there to help her and felt responsible for what she had become, my friends felt bad when I said this, and it made my friend Marvin say, "It's not your fault."

"In some ways, it is," I began. "But I am willing to make up for it like Rain just did for Cordelia."

After we were done talking, we all went back into the tent. None of us went back to sleep even though we had Rain's word that she wouldn't send anyone after us. We all wondered how long it would take for the people of Drainton City to discover that we had already passed through. But we soon remembered that if we were caught, our friends at the Magical Mountain Manor would do something about it. But we still had to ensure we could reach the treasure without any trouble, plus I knew a few spells, so all in all, if anyone wanted to mess with us, they needed to prepare to pay a big price.

6

The Last Challenges

It took us almost until the afternoon to get up and set off once again, and because of this, I wasn't sure how far we would get before the day was over. I also wondered if Rain would keep her word and not tell the people of Drainton City about us. Because the last thing we needed was any other witches and wizards trying to stop us from completing our journey to the treasure. But Cordelia helped put it out of my mind for the time being, because it was not important as long as no one came after us.

However, after an hour passed as we walked on, we soon reached the Lava Ponds, and it was this area that made us very worried. This was because there was barely a way to get across. There was also a sign that said,

If you fall into the lava you'll be gone forever.

Also, this area reminded us of being in a volcano, but luckily, this was not a volcano. But with all the shaking and rumbling going on, we were not so sure; in fact, I almost had a feeling that magic had something to do with it being the way it was. All the same, as I looked in every direction, I was beginning to think we just hit a dead end. Getting around this place would take all day, maybe longer, but it looked like there was no way to cross this thing. But just when I was about to have an idea, my friend Andria said, "So how are we going to get across?"

As she said this, the ground beneath us started to shake, and a lot harder, too, which was why I now said, "Well, there is one way across this, but I really don't want to do this in front of Cordelia."

"Alex!" Talia began in anger. "Are you saying the only way we're going to get across is to use magic?"

Everyone was getting angry at this, and just when I was about to say something, Cordelia then said, "I don't care if you use magic if it is our only option." I tried to say something, but she cut through and said, "Alex, I don't care anymore that I can't do magic, and I don't care if you do it in front of me. But I would like to know how you got magic in the first place."

I was afraid she was going to say that, but I told her this was not the time to tell it since it was a long story. All the same, after I got out my wand and pointed it at the lava, I then said in a very loud voice, "Creates, pathless, appearess!"

At my spell, a six-foot-long path came out of the lava, and keeping a tight grip on my wand, all six of us walked across. The walk across was not easy because not only was the ground beginning to shake again, and worse than ever, but the lava even began to spill onto the path. Once or twice one of us almost fell into the lava. If I hadn't cast another spell at that moment, we might have died right there and then. When we finally got across the path disappeared.

After I caught my breath and stowed my wand away I said, "Well, guys, the only thing left before we reach the treasure is the Haunted Dark Forest."

"And then we can go home?" Andria said, feeling happy, and it allowed me to say, "Yes, when we find the treasure and get as much as we want, we'll get to go home where new lives await us. Because we'll become richer than anyone could ever hope to be and maybe show the one percent what people should really do with their fortune."

Everyone exchanged looks when I said this, and my friend Eddy said, "So how far is the forest from here?"

"Just ten miles," I said.

"Alex!" Cordelia began in a sad voice, and when I turned to her, she went on and said, making me feel a bit nervous as she spoke, "Are you sure you want to go through that forest? They say you'll never feel the same again once you face your worst fears. And sometimes your fears can scare you into a state that will never let you move again."

I knew this might come since she did grow up in this world, meaning she knew so much that we didn't. But the thing I said to her, hoping she would see reason was, "Cordelia, if we want to reach the treasure and go home, we have no choice but to pass through that forest. But I do have a plan, and with any luck, we'll make it through. I just hope we do it before it gets dark."

"Why's that?" Talia said, which now made me say, "Do you guys really want to spend the night in a haunted forest?"

"He's got a point!" Cordelia began. "Because no one has ever come out of that forest or felt the same after spending the night."

They all knew we were right, and after seeing this, I now said, "Okay, let's keep moving."

It wasn't long until we got to the forest and saw that the whole forest was covered by a dark sky. Plus, all the trees looked dead and scary-looking, and it felt like we were about to walk into a nightmare. The only one who was really afraid was Cordelia, which was why she grabbed one of my arms as we got closer. And the thing I said in a voice only she could hear was, "As long as we stick together, nothing will hurt us."

This made her say, "I will be fine; just lead the way like you have done so far, Alex."

When we came to the entrance of the forest, a large sign with red blood-like writing hanging on a tree, said,

If I were you I would not go in.

We ignored this and walked in, even saw in a very far distance the light at the end, meaning this might be a while. However, just when we were five feet in, an evil, cackling voice, called out of nowhere and said, "What are the six of you doing in my forest?"

"We're just passing through," I said as I got my wand out, because I knew we were in for one hell of a time even as I went on and said, "You got a problem with that?"

I thought I proved our point to whatever this was, but it did not give up so easily, and the thing it said now was, "You have no right passing through my forest; no one has any right to pass through my forest. Now, get out before I unleash my dark magic on you, magic that you cannot take on and will be your end."

At that, I said with so much courage in my voice and ready to cast a spell at whatever came next, "We're passing through with or without your permission, and if you think you can mess with us, you're wrong."

After this, I thought we finally got through to it, but the dark voice laughed at us and then said, "You and your friends are making a big mistake, boy, and you'll be sorry for messing with someone like me."

We laughed at this, and then I said, "That's strong talk for someone who won't show themselves. Or are you afraid to come and face us?"

"Was that supposed to be a threat, boy?" the voice said.

I gave a cruel smile before saying, "Maybe it was if you know what a threat is."

"You have spirit, boy. But we'll see how strong and brave you all are when you face the dark magic of my forest."

We didn't hear this part because I was whispering a plan to the others, and then I said in a cheeky voice, "I'm sorry, can you repeat that?"

This made this voice very angry and it let out a loud growl, but when it repeated itself, I then said, "Well, we'll see that for ourselves."

At that, I gave the others the sign and all six of us began running as fast as we could to the other end. And as we ran and kept to the path that led to the other end of the forest, the dark voice laughed and then said, "You think the six of you can escape and get to the other end of my forest? You're wrong."

As he said this, ten monster-looking ghosts started swooping down at us, causing a few of us to scream and me to wave my wand and say, "Airflow!"

At that spell the ghosts spun out of control and out of sight. I did this a few times since more and more ghosts kept coming toward us. I even used many other spells to keep them away. We kept running as many more ghosts came at us, and as we ran, we hoped we were almost out of the forest.

Unfortunately, we still had a long way before we reached the end, and just as we turned a corner, two evil-looking trees started to come toward us and blocked our way, and we backed away, but there were more behind us as well. That prompted me to say to all the trees, "Stopper!" And that caused them to freeze in time, and then I used more magic to push them away, which allowed us to pass by.

When we started to see light ahead, we were grateful, but it didn't allow us to slow down. But just when we almost made it, an ugly-looking clown appeared out of nowhere and, like the trees, blocked our way out. And just as it came toward us, more clowns appeared. The dark voice to then laughed, "Try using your magic on that, boy."

I laughed back at the voice when it said this and then said, "Oh, I will!" I then pointed my wand and said a few times to all the clowns, "Blaster!" And that caused the clowns to be blasted five feet away and out of the forest, allowing us to reach the end. The clowns turned to dust when they were close to the sunlight, and we finally got out of the forest at the other end.

As we were a few inches away, the dark voice then said, "You six are strong, very strong, but if you ever come back this way, and I know you will, I'll be ready, and next time, you won't leave my forest alive, you hear me? The next time I see the six of you, the next time you pass through my forest, you will not leave my forest alive."

To that, we all turned back and said at the top of our voices, "Shut up!"

As we walked on, the voice of the forest said in a whining and defeated voice, "I hate those six."

When we were as far as we wanted from the forest, we saw that it was halfway between the afternoon and the evening, and I thought to myself that maybe, just maybe, we might reach the treasure today. This thought kept me happy inside my head, and just when I was about to say this to the others, flashes of light began shooting down at us. I knew even before we saw them that we were under attack since no one was around but us and they were not shooting in any other direction but ours.

The ones who attacked us were a witch and a wizard on broomsticks flying a few feet away from the forest. Their aim was not that great because they kept missing us, but when I saw my chance, I cast a spell on them both. The spell I cast was strong, too, because not only did it blast their wands out of their hands, but it also caused them to fall off their brooms and crash onto the ground not that far from where we were.

Luckily, they were not killed, which was something I was not trying to do, but they were knocked out. As we approached them, Cordelia almost fainted, and she had every reason, because this witch and wizard couple were her parents.

The witch had the same hairstyle as Cordelia's, but shorter and with green highlights. She also had a stern face and wore dark black witch's robes but didn't wear a witch's hat. As for the wizard, who was Cordelia's father, he had a gray mustache and hair with a friendly face and had a stern but untidy style of wizard's robes. After Cordelia told us who they were, we all looked worried.

Nevertheless, the thing I said as I got my wand ready, because I thought there might be a fight coming was, "Why are they out here? I thought your sister gave us her word that she wasn't going to tell anyone about us."

"I thought so, too!" Cordelia said feeling worried and uneasy at the same time, "Because Rain never breaks her word or any promise she makes to anyone no matter what the situation is."

A moment of silence followed, and when they began to stir, I cast a spell that caused unbreakable ropes to tie them up and then said as they were tied back-to-back to each other was, "Well, let's ask why they are out here and why they were trying to kill us."

No one replied, and as they woke up, Cordelia said with a bit of anger in her voice and feeling a bit uneasy, "Why are you two out here?"

The one who answered was the wizard, and he said in a calm but sorrowful voice, "We heard that the travelers got past the city."

"And now it's just something to laugh about," the witch said, and when she wanted to continue, the wizard then instead went on and said, "Because if five strangers can pass through without detection, there must be a reason they came for the treasure." He then chuckled before saying, "How did you kids do it?"

"We have our ways!" I said, which made the witch and wizard laugh. Then the witch said, looking at the situation she and her husband were in and feeling a bit uneasy as she spoke, "Question: Why did you tie us up?"

"Well, why did you attack us?" I said.

"Watch your tone, boy," Cordelia's father said then continued on, "And we were not trying to attack or even kill any of you; we were trying to get your attention."

"So we can say goodbye to our daughter," Cordelia's mother said, which made Cordelia say, "You came out here."

"Cordelia!" her mother said. "I know we failed as your parents because we honored our pride and never saw what it was doing to you."

"And we're sorry," her father said, and just when Cordelia was about to say something, her father went on and said, "And if you really want to do what you're doing, we support it if it means you can finally find happiness."

Cordelia never expected them to do anything like this, which was why she now said, feeling a bit bad as she spoke, "Never thought running away would cause you to do this, which is why I don't think I can."

"We don't expect you to," her mother said. "We just wanted to say goodbye and hope you find the life you are looking for, Cordelia."

This caused me to untie them, and after saying goodbye, Cordelia's father asked if he could talk to me in private. I was not keen on it, but I still did, and after

I was out of earshot of the others, he then said, "My other daughter Rain told me that there is another reason she is running away with you and your friends."

I didn't answer because I was afraid of what he would do to me; nevertheless, he then smiled at me and said, "Well, boy, let me just say you'd better keep her happy, the very thing I failed to do."

"I promise I will," I said.

"That-a-boy!" her father said, and then he and his wife got back on their brooms and flew back to Drainton City.

After I got back to the others, we pressed on. As we walked Cordelia asked me what her father wanted with me. And I just told her he hoped she would be happy in our world.

After a few minutes, one of my friends asked if we might reach the treasure today, and the thing I said was, "We might if we keep moving."

"That's a good thing!" Talia began with a yawn. "Because I want to go home."

"I think that is what we all want," I said. And the second I finished this, we found ourselves standing right outside of a blocked up cave.

7

The Treasure of the Ancient Wizards

We knew even without the map popping out of my pocket and back in again that we were finally here. We finally made it to the place where the Treasure of the Ancient Wizards was kept and waiting for us. After all this time, after many, many days of traveling through this world, we were finally at our destination. As we stared at the blocked up cave, we noticed it was starting to get dark, but we didn't care. None of us were tired, and what was the point of making camp and sleeping for the night when we finally made it to our destination, finally came to the end of this adventure? And so, after being a foot away, I said the same spell I had used on the clowns back in the forest, and it made us a clear path into the cave.

As we were walking in, many torches began lighting the place up, and not just on the cave walls, but on the cave ceilings as well, and this gave us enough light to see where we were going. Also, the second we were all in the cave, it sealed itself back up, leaving no way out, which was not our problem right now, because all we wanted was to reach the end and see what awaited us.

It wasn't long until we did. As we were walking, I could see the keyhole up ahead, and it really excited all of us. But before I did anything, I turned to the others and said, "Well, guys, we finally made it, and now, let's go and get what we've wanted to get after many weeks of traveling."

I turned back to the wall, took off my key necklace for the first time since this adventure had started, placed it in the hole, and twisted it a few times. Then the key and the wall disappeared. This made us happy… until it revealed a stairway leading down.

"What?" I said, both shocked and angry. "This was not on the map."

"Maybe!" Cordelia began as she tried to calm me down. "The treasure is all the way down there."

And no sooner did she say this then more torches began lighting the way down to who knows where, as if activated by her voice. This disappointed me and made me say, "Well, that's what I think, too, but if I knew we still had a long way to go, we might be relaxing by a fire right now, even eating a really great meal and sleeping right now."

At this, my four best friends started saying things like,

"But Alex, none of us are tired."

"And we're finally here, so what's the point of turning back now or even spending another night in this world?"

"And with the caves blocked up, do you really want to repeat your spell over and over again?"

"They're right, Alex," Cordelia began as she took my hand. "Why should we turn back when we are so close to this treasure? Yes, we still have one more thing to face, but we are still almost there, and there really is no point in stopping now."

I was glad to hear all this, and it made me say in a happy voice as a few tears came into my eyes, "Well, guys, it's decided: We'll continue on and end our adventure right here and now. But before we go on, I have something I'd like to say, something I wish I'd said to all a long time ago."

"What's that?" all five of them said, and after I took a deep breath, I then said, letting go of Cordelia's hand and stepping back, "Well, before we started this adventure, I was all forth on doing this alone; I was not keen on allowing you guys to come at all because of the danger. But now I see I did the right thing by bringing you all with me, and this is something to remember for the rest of our lives."

I paused because I was hoping someone would say something, but when no one did, I went on and said, "All of you have been the greatest friends anyone could ever hope to have. I couldn't ask for better. I'm also glad we found and saved a new friend from a sad and miserable life and brought her with us." Cordelia blushed at this, and then I said to her, "Cordelia, you are a wonderful non-witch that this world never got a chance to know you properly, and I am glad your family allowed this."

"The only good thing they've ever done," she said.

"Nevertheless," I said before she could go on, "when you come back with us to our world, many good people will see what the people of this world should have seen from the start."

"Thank you, Alex!" she said as she turned red.

I smiled at this and then said with so much greatness and gratitude swelling in my voice, "And now, my friends, let's go and get what we came here for."

And so we all began walking down, but after a few seconds, we were all starting to get tired because this stairway looked like it could never end, and it was not just stairs we were walking down, because there were a lot of twists and turns whenever we thought we came to the end, and when the others asked if there was a spell for this, I said, "I'm sorry, guys, but there isn't a spell for this. I wish there was; otherwise, we would be there in no time."

"That stinks!" Marvin said.

"Well, guys," I said feeling a bit annoyed, "magic can't be used for everything; otherwise, life is just plain lazy, something we all know too well."

"He's right," Cordelia said.

As the others could feel their legs beginning to ache, which was why they started to get mad at me and Cordelia for saying this, but we were right: You can't use magic for everything, and sometimes, in a lot of situations, magic can make things worse. But that seems to always happen when you want to take the easy way out, which a lot of companies do and which causes more problems than anything else.

All the same, as we kept walking on, I began to think we might break through the center of this world or at least go all the way down to the end of it since there seemed to be no end. As this thought came into my mind we came to a small long tunnel that was so hard to walk through, and a few times, a few of us got stuck. We needed a lot of wiggling and creativity to get through with our bags.

Nevertheless, just when I was about to say something or see if this was on the map, my friend Talia said, "Are we there yet?"

"We'll get there when we get there," I said, beginning to feel annoyed and tired at the same time as we now came to another flight of stairs leading down. I felt a little how a father must feel on a long drive. "Just calm down, everyone. I know this is taking longer than expected, but things don't always happen at the time you want them to."

"Sorry, Alex!" Talia said again. "It's just that this stairway looks like it will never end."

"I know it looks that way," I said feeling frustrated. "But I do believe we are almost there." And the second I said this, we finally came to the end of this stairway, and at first we were grateful until we saw—which only made my friends disappointed and led to a good bit of groaning—another wall blocking any way through, in, or out.

"I can't believe this," Marvin said.

"Yeah, we came all this way for nothing," Eddy finished, and before anyone could say another word, I held up a hand for silence and said, "Everyone, just calm down. I don't think we hit a dead end."

"What makes you say that, Alex?" Cordelia said, and at the same time, I came toward the wall and saw something that put a smile on my face and made me say as I got out the map, "Well, I know I've seen this done many times in books and movies, and I always wondered if there was more to this map since it is shaped just a bit oddly, but maybe, just maybe…"

So I smoothed out the map and placed it on a shape that resembled it, and after I backed away, the whole wall glowed bright gold, which caused us all to cover our eyes since it was so bright. But it didn't matter, because it only lasted a short second, and after the light brightened the whole area, the wall disappeared and revealed a chamber, a chamber we were hoping to find since this started.

The treasure in the chamber was filled with billions and billions of golden and strange-looking coins. There were even five waterfalls which were on the very end of the chamber walls, and each one of them was pouring down billions and billions of golden and strange coins, and the source of where it was coming from was unknown. There were not just golden strange coins covering each part of this chamber and other areas we saw when we entered, but many other valuables, even valuables that had not been seen in a long time and others you might see in other areas in the world. Nevertheless, these valuables the treasure chamber had were diamonds and sapphires of all different sizes along with jeweled and ruby crowns and tiaras, even gold and silver chairs, thrones, suits of armor, statues, staffs, weapons, and golden nuggets. I thought that was all at first, but then we saw silver, pearls, and jewels of all kinds, many different gems, rings of all sizes, and many others as well, things I didn't even know about.

Marvin, Andria, Talia, and Eddy were the ones who ran in first and started gathering as much as they could, even danced in joy and excitement because of this place being so awe inspiring. They managed to stuff a lot of this, not only in the sacks I gave them before this all started, but in their pockets as well, and they all went a bit wild as they touched and gathered a lot of this treasure. Thankfully it was just excitement and not true gold fever. But that was indeed something to prepare for in a place like this, and as this was happening, I was looking around the whole chamber.

I still couldn't believe we were finally here, and though I was amazed, I was still able to take a few steps in, dropped to my knees, and said in a voice which sounded like it was breaking and never used as I gathered as much of the treasure as I could in my hands, feeling like this was the best moment of my life, "After all these years and many, many days of traveling, I can touch it, feel it in my hands. At long last, the Treasure of the Ancient Wizards is in my sights and in my hands and all around me."

After I got over my own gold fever, which took a while to do, I started looking for Cordelia, and when I saw her, I was sad because she was standing by a corner alone. She also looked the same way she did when I first met her in that alley in Drainton City, which was why I went over to ask her what was wrong.

She said as she looked away from me, "Oh, nothing, Alex. I'm just feeling happy for you all."

"But you don't look happy," I said.

And when I put a hand on her shoulder, she then said, "Well, seeing you all go crazy about this place is making me think that you might not be taking—"

"Of course we're going to take you back with us," I said before she could finish. "We're not leaving here without you, because that will be breaking a promise, and we don't do things like that." She tried to say something, but I then said, "We're just happy we finally found this place, because we've been wanting to get here for a very long time."

Cordelia felt a bit better when I said this and then said, as she turned to face me and wiped a few tears out of her eyes, "I guess I'm being a bit selfish seeing you all happy because of this place, something—"

"It's okay!" I began feeling a bit nervous as I now said, "But you know what made me happy before we even came here?"

"What's that?" she said feeling like she knew the answer but shocked at the same time.

"Meeting you!" I said. Though this seemed to stun her, it still allowed me to say, as I took her hand while her eyes gazed into mine, "Ever since I met you in that alleyway in Drainton City, Cordelia, I felt something I've never felt before, something I know I could never feel if I never met you, because you're the most beautiful and—"

"Are you saying you're in love with me?" she cut in, and how much I wanted to say "Yes," but the words wouldn't come out no matter how hard I tried. Instead, she grabbed me by the head and kissed me full on the mouth, and I kissed her back, and we only broke apart just so she could say, "I'm in love with you, too."

That filled me up with so much happiness, which was why I kissed her again, and there was nothing more wonderful than the feel of Cordelia's lips on mine and having my hands on her back. This was a moment I didn't want ending, but unfortunately, it did, because after a few seconds, my friends came over and said as they were covered with and holding as much of this treasure as they could, "Oh, how romantic!"

I was mad at them for spoiling the greatest moment of my life, and after they all said they were sorry, they asked if I was going to get any of the treasure for myself. And that allowed me to say as both Cordelia and I began walking around the chamber, holding hands as we did so, "I am, and whatever I get, it's going to be both mine and Cordelia's."

"It doesn't have to be!" she said with a giggle, which allowed me to now say, as I blushed another bright color, "Yes, it should."

Both she and I smiled at each other as we said this, and what my friend Marvin now said was, "You're serious, Alex?"

"You're going to share what you get with your girlfriend?" Andria added, and I said kissing Cordelia on the cheeks as I spoke, "Yes, I am!"

And just when Cordelia and I were about to kiss again, a voice echoed all over the chamber and said, "Well said, Alex, well said."

Of course, I knew this was the voice of the wizard, but what surprised me was when my friends said at different times and looking around at the same time, "What was that?"

At that second, which caused me to let go of Cordelia's hand, the wizard appeared out of nowhere. He clapped his hands and walked up toward us at the same time, "Well done, my friends, well done. You finally found the Treasure of the Ancient Wizards."

Everyone but me was surprised at this, and when they all asked him who he was, he stopped clapping and stood where he was, then pointed to me, "Why don't you ask Alex who I am?" He murmured amicably.

They all turned to me and started saying things like,

"You know this guy!"

"How does he know you?"

"Why didn't you tell us about this man?"

"How did he know we would end up here?"

"Have you been keeping any other secrets from us?"

"Yes, have you?"

Before they could say another word, I then said, hoping this would help and feeling a bit uneasy as I spoke, "Guys, the reason I never told you that this is the wizard who has been helping us through this whole adventure was because I didn't think you would believe me if I told you."

"Why would you think we wouldn't believe you?" Talia said.

"Alex!" Marvin began. "We've seen enough things in this world to know anything is possible, no matter what it is."

"I know that!" I began putting a hand to my forehead. "But not only has he been talking to me in my head since all this began, but he only appeared in a dream I had back at the Magical Mountain Manor and when he stopped time after I told Cordelia she could come with us, which was why I thought no one would believe me if I said anything about it."

"He's right, my friends," the wizard began. "No one, not even anyone in this world, would ever believe what I did to Alex here. And even if he did tell you, you would say you believed him, but you would also say behind his back that he was going crazy."

"We would never think he was going crazy," Andria said with a stern look.

Just when the wizard was about to say something to this, my friend Talia said, "But why did you only appear to Alex and not the rest of us?"

The wizard chuckled at this before saying, "Because it was him and him alone that had to pass the task I set for all of you to prove you were worthy to have this treasure, which you all have done, and now this all belongs to you; it no longer belongs to me."

Him saying this made me almost say something, but then I remembered something I had read in the book called **The History of the Magicalworld**, and what our friends from the Magical Mountain Manor were whispering about when I told them how I knew everything I needed to know about this world, which was why I now burst out and said, "You're one of the Ancient Wizards, aren't you?"

The wizard smiled at me when I said this and then said, "I am, my boy, and I'm glad you finally figured that out."

I felt embarrassed when he said this, and what I said now was, "Well, I had a feeling I knew the whole time, but I wasn't so sure if I was right."

Everyone laughed at this, and when the wizard held out a hand for silence, he then said, as he summoned one of the chairs for him to sit on, "Well, my boy, you don't always have to know everything to begin an adventure or if you really want to do something great with your life."

"But may I ask you something?" I asked him.

"Ask away," the wizard said.

It took me a while to say this because I was wondering if I chose my words carefully; all the same, the thing I said now was, "Well, sir, why did you want us to have this treasure in the first place if it's rightfully yours?"

This put a sad and slightly distant look on the wizard's face as he now said, "Because all this treasure does, my young friend I've watched grow, is remind me that I don't have brothers or sisters anymore, and it does me no good. That's why I chose you to have it, Alex, because you're a boy who is loyal to all those you care about and brave against those who make your and your friends' lives a living nightmare. Plus, you're kind to those who deserve it and know the right people to trust. That's why you and your friends deserve this treasure, and I hope you will use it for the right reasons."

"And we do plan on using it for the right reasons," Andria said, nodding, and the wizard then gave her a stern look, "Please explain."

And so we told him everything we had told our friends at the Magical Mountain Manor, and when we finished, the wizard then said with a smile on his face, "Well, this means I have indeed chosen wisely, because if that's what you plan on using the treasure for, then you deserve every last bit of it. As for the people in Drainton City, you don't have to worry about them because they now see this is not something worth protection if the kids after it managed to pass by without being noticed."

We all laughed at this, and then after a few seconds, he got up, walked past us, and said, "But I think we've talked enough; right now, the thing I want the six of you to do is hold out your sacks so I can give you every last bit of this treasure."

"We can't!" I said without thinking, and what the wizard said to me was, "And why is that?"

"Well, sir," I said beginning to feel a bit worried, "everyone but me has already filled up their sacks and pockets, and there is no more room for it all. Also, Cordelia doesn't have a sack, and I promised her I would share what I get with her."

The wizard chuckled at this, then said coming up to me, "Oh, but aren't you forgetting, my dear boy, that anything is possible with just a bit of magic?"

This allowed me to say in an excited voice, "Do you mean—?"

"I do!" he said before I could finish, going on by saying, "But to do it, I need my wand back, and if you please, may I have it back, Alex?"

These were the last words I ever expected to hear. All the same, I took out the wand and said before handing it to him, "This is your wand."

"It is, my boy!" He began feeling a bit bad when he saw the look on my face and went on by saying, "And before you found it along with all the other stuff that started all this, I put a spell on it allowing it to work on the first human it touches, giving them magic of their own until the wand is back in its true owner's hands. And now, please, Alex, I don't want to ask you again."

So, I gave the wand to him, and the second that happened, a small ball of red, yellow, blue, and green lights of energy shot out of my body and zapped right into the wizard.

"I am sorry, my young friend, I know how much you enjoyed doing magic, but it's not meant for your kind to learn our ways." He patted my shoulder lightly.

"It's all right," I said beginning to feel a bit sad and getting something out of my rucksack at the same time. "But do you want the books back, too?"

"Oh, no!" he said sealing my rucksack and going on by saying, "You may keep those as long as you never show them to another living soul as long as you live."

To that, I nodded and said, "I promise, and I wish I could give you back the chest."

"But you sold it," the wizard said with a smile before I could finish, then went on and said, "to pay for the things you needed to get through this whole world and more."

"How did you know about that?" I said in a surprised voice.

The wizard just said, with a bit of mischief in his eyes and voice, "Because I was the one who bought it back from you." I was shocked and was about to say something, but he went on and said, "The day when you realized you needed money for all this, I not only pointed you in the right direction but also ensured you couldn't know we had met face-to-face on that day. But I did it so you could not only get what you needed for you and your friends, but also so I could get one thing back before someone found it and caused many to stop you and your friends from having what was the best adventure you ever had."

"But why didn't you tell me that was you on that day?" I said.

The wizard chuckled and then said, "Because it was not the right time for you or any of your friends to know just yet; you had to wait until the time was right."

Though this all confused us, it didn't stop him from looking around a few times and then saying, "But that's enough for now." He then gave a small flick with his wand, which made another sack appear for Cordelia, then said a very powerful and hard-to-say spell as he swished it around four times, which caused everything in the chamber, our sacks, and our pockets to rise up into the air. Everything then spun around a few times, first in slow motion, then in fast motion, and then dropped in our sacks like heavy raindrops. When the last thing dropped into our sacks, they tied themselves up and they all started hovering a few feet from the ground and next to us. We then looked around the chamber and saw it was now completely empty, which was a real shock, because knowing that everything which was once in this chamber was now in our sacks was a real surprise indeed.

After the wizard was done with this, he then said, "Well, my friends, the time has come for me to take you all back to the Humanworld."

"We're going home?" Eddy said, which caused the wizard to smile and say, "Oh, yes, and just so you all know, this is your first and your last adventure in this world."

"Wait!" Andria said in a shocked voice. "Are you saying we can never come back?"

"That's the way it has to be," the wizard said uneasily.

We were all surprised and sad about this, and Talia said sadly, "But we have to come back; we promised our friends at the Magical Mountain Manor that we would come back one day."

"You can't expect us to break a promise to them," Andria said, finishing this all up.

And just before any one of us could say another word, the wizard then said, "I understand your concerns, and I'm very sorry about it, too. But there are promises you keep and promises you break, and this is a promise you have no choice but to break. I know they will understand after I tell them, but they know as well as I do that if you keep coming to this world, and if more of your kind follow in the process, there is a possibility like you were told before that you will be caught and be experimented on, which is something that cannot be allowed to happen."

"He's right, guys," Cordelia added. "Even I don't want that happening to you."

"Spoken like a true friend, Cordelia," he said, and then he went on as he gathered us all together. "But now the time has come to take you home, so…" He then pointed his wand to the ceiling and said, "Teleportess motuss!"

And to that, the treasure chamber was gone, and we were now traveling through something that looked like hyperspace.

8

The Ending

W**e were now** standing in the middle room of my parents' house, and we were happy until we saw what was happening after we came into focus. This is because each one of our parents was in the living room, and they were all crying their eyes out. When we made a sound to say we were here, they all looked in our direction and ran right toward us, and after a few minutes of hugging, they began saying things like,

"Where have you kids been all this time?"

"You know how worried we've all been?"

"We had the police and everyone looking for all five of you."

"And who are these two?"

"And why do you have sacks filled with who knows what?"

And just when another one of our parents was about to say something, the wizard held out his hand for silence and said, "Calm yourselves, everyone; all your questions will be answered if you all return to the living room and have a seat."

And so they all did, and just when everyone was about to sit, a door leading to the stairway and above opened, and my sister walked through it, along with a girl who had her arms wrapped around her. She had a shocked expression on her face like she'd seen a ghost, but when she ran up to me and hugged me, she said as she began to cry, "Do you know how worried I have been? I thought you were—"

"Please, young lady," the wizard said before she could finish, and when my sister returned to this girl, everyone but us sat down because we were standing behind the wizard and hoping he would help them understand. After ensuring everyone was listening and calm, he told them everything from leading me to the chest, to allowing my friends to come with me, to why

I acted so strange for a couple of years. When he got to the part about why he wanted us to have this treasure in the first place, my mother said in an angry voice, "So what you are saying is that you led my son and his friends to find a treasure you wanted to give away and made them learn so much about another world to keep them alive?"

"That is true, ma'am," he said trying to keep calm in the room.

But it didn't stop my father from saying, "But if you wanted our kids to have this treasure so much, why didn't you just give it to them?"

The wizard chuckled at this and then said, "Because they needed to prove to themselves and to me that they were worthy to have this treasure, which they have done. Also, it wouldn't be wise to give away something like this so easily."

"That may be true," my sister said, "but four years had passed, and we thought they were all dead, so—"

"And I will have something done about it," the wizard said before my sister could finish, and then he went on and said, "Because they will be richer than anyone could ever hope to be, and something like this needs a good cover story. However," the wizard said as he saw the looks on our parents' faces and the looks my sister and this girl were giving us, "you will not punish your kids for everything they have done, and you will not, I repeat, not take any of their treasure unless you have their permission, and I will know if you try, understand?"

When no one answered, the wizard turned back to us and said, "Well, my friends, your adventure is now over, but there are a few things to say before I leave you. And the first thing to say is, please open your sacks and see what is inside them now."

And so we did, and a few seconds later, everything in them turned into piles of one-hundred-dollar bills, and that is what made me ask, "How did that happen?"

The wizard smiled and then said, "It's a spell I put on it long ago, so when the treasure enters your world, it will all turn into the kind of money you use here. And another thing to say is, no matter how much you use, even if it is for yourselves or for others, it will never get any lower since this magic will allow it to stay the same as if you never used it in the first place. Every year on this day, your treasure will triple itself, making you richer than you already are. But, this magic will only last if you and your descendants use it to do a lot of good and not what so many rich people in this world do today."

Of course, we were never going to do what many rich people do today; it was one of the reasons I was afraid to become rich. But we all planned to do a lot of good, something rich people never like to do, and that will probably earn us a lot of enemies with them. All the same, the wizard saw these thoughts in my head, which was why he now said, "I have chosen right, and now I say goodbye, but be sure, we will meet again in the near future."

And with that, he disappeared. When he was gone, we said we were sorry for all the worry we had caused them all. After they said we were forgiven, one of our parents said, "So how rich are you kids?"

We all exchanged different looks before I said, "We're richer than anyone can ever hope to be, and we can buy and do whatever we want, and I do mean anything."

"Well, bro, I guess that means you can buy me whatever I want," my sister said.

I knew this was coming sooner or later, which was why I now said, "Wow, that's not something new."

"Hey!" she said taking a step toward me. "You have been gone for four years and—"

"And just so you know," I said before she could finish, "there was a time I wanted you to come, but since we were drifting apart and you were in with the in-crowd—"

"So basically, I missed a chance to go on a great adventure?"

A moment of silence followed, and then the thing I said to her was, "But I am sorry I never told you about any of this or even made you think I shut you out."

My sister then looked down and said, as this girl she was with came and held her, "I will admit when you disappeared, I was deadly worried, even dropped a lot of my friends believing that might bring you back, but if it wasn't for my girlfriend here, I might have lost it completely."

"Well, I'm sorry," I said feeling bad. "But even if I did tell you, you might not believe me because you don't believe in magic."

"Well, I do now," she said.

Both of us laughed, and just when one of us was about to say something else, my mother jumped in and said while looking at Cordelia, "Well, we do wish you did tell us something like this, but one thing I would like to know now is… who is this girl you brought back with you?"

At that, Cordelia stepped forth, said her name, and went on by saying, "I'm a non-witch from the Magicalworld and…" She took my hand when she said this last part: "I'm your son's girlfriend."

At her words, both my mother and my sister began teasing me, something I never enjoy from either them or my father, and my sister said, laughing as she did so, "Oh, so you found yourself a girlfriend on this adventure of yours, uh, Alex?"

After giving her a look that said that was enough, I then turned to Cordelia and said as we both smiled at each other, "Well, they always say one day you'll find the right person you want to spend the rest of your life with. And Cordelia is not just that; she is also the perfect girl for me."

We were just about to kiss when the wizard's voice echoed all over the room and said, "And that is another reason I sent you to the Magicalworld, my boy."

I was amazed that he was still doing this and glad I was not the only one hearing him, which was why I could now say, "You mean you wanted me to meet Cordelia, sir?"

"That is true, Alex!" the wizard said still echoing through the room. "And this is because you were never going to find the right girl in this world, which I'm sorry to say, that is. And Cordelia was never going to be happy in the Magicalworld, which I'm sorry to say to you, Cordelia. But I thought the both of you would make a grand couple."

"And you were right, sir," I said still looking for the source. "Too bad she will live—"

"Oh, I would not say that, my friend," the wizard said before I could continue, and when I asked what he meant, he went on and said, "Well, my friend, if you and your friends stayed in the Magicalworld, you would live forever, and now that Cordelia lives here—"

"Meaning she is not immortal anymore," I said without thinking, and just when I was about to say something, she then said, feeling both uneasy and happy at the same time, "Which I am very okay with as long as I have you by my side, Alex."

"Well said!" the wizard said again, and after that, he was completely gone.

Years had now passed, and we were all living the good life, and we didn't take advantage of it as many other rich people do. Also, the wizard managed to give us a grand cover story on how we became richer than anyone could ever hope to be. It was on the news three weeks after our adventure came to an end, and what one of the anchorpeople said on one of the news channels was, "In our top story today, the five missing kids have returned."

"It turns out," the second anchorperson said, "They have been traveling to a far and unknown area of America and found a treasure no one ever knew existed, and here is what one of our field reporters has to say."

And to that, they changed the screen to our hometown and a young reporter saying, in a happy but serious voice, "These five are not telling us how they managed to uncover this treasure. But I will say that no rich person alive today can compare to what these kids now have."

More was said on this and many other news channels, plus this helped us avoid questions with the IRS. And since we paid our own taxes and added a lot of extras, they never tried to breathe down our necks. The things we had now were very large manor houses with a lot of land and beautiful landscapes, and the good things we did for many people, since it was not just the promise we had made to the wizard but to ourselves as well, included building in each country around the world grand houses for the homeless, the poor, and anyone that couldn't afford to live or get a place of their own. We even made sure the economy never went wrong again, even had new companies to give many people jobs. We built and owned a lot of places as well, even ensured the wrong people never had a place in the government ever again, even changed a lot of the rules in the government to ensure many people could be treated as equals, and so the wrong people were never allowed to carry a gun again. That was something we had to work hard to change by getting the people who wanted it to happen in the right places, because people needed to feel safe, even if many disagreed. And we did earn a lot of enemies with the corrupted trying to seize power again, but many with the upper class, because they thought what we were doing was not the way to go, and we just insulted them and said they didn't care about anyone but themselves.

We did use some of the treasure to treat ourselves and our families to a grand life and ensure many could achieve this as well. Also, I never knew almost everything my friends did, but the things I did were not only pay for my parents' retirements, but got them vacation homes in Florida, Hawaii, and the Caribbean Islands and ensured they were nowhere near mine. I even spoiled them rotten every chance I got, and I had a lot of chances, too. I did a lot for my sister, too, even got her into the best schools in the world. Even though she did forgive me for not letting her in on everything that made all this possible, I still thought I needed to make up for it, and she enjoyed these schools she went to better than public schools, because not only was she the top student in her classes, but she was also recommended to every college on this planet.

Moving on, other things I did were buy and tear down the middle school and high school I hated so much. I built grand areas for kids of all ages in their places, places to eat and hang out, and even to show there is more to life than getting into trouble. But the best thing I did in my opinion, of course, was build on an island I owned a grand boarding school. This school was to bring kids from all over the world together, and it soon put many other schools out of service, which was not my intention, but to show many that they may be different in some ways, but alike in others ways. It helped bring world peace, a goal I had hoped to see happen even before I became so rich.

But as I was saying, because this island was so big and was a barren rock when I found it, I was not only able to make this school into the biggest building ever with large classes of every subject known or ever taught, I also made sure it was run by teachers that were not unfair and cruel like many teachers of this day are. Nevertheless, this school was not just so children around the world could learn something more, but to enjoy themselves when they didn't need to study. This school had a large swimming pool with a few good waterslides, an arcade with every game ever made, a very large movie theater that played any movie you wanted, even movies already out, a few good restaurants with really good food from around the world, and spots to shop. Also, this was not just for students to enjoy themselves, but to work and earn not just money for themselves, but credit for what they wanted to do after they entered their final year. And I even ensured the prices on these places were a very low amount.

There was so much more I did for many others, but I always found time to enjoy myself. And when the years began to pass, my friends and I went our separate ways but still stayed in touch with one another. And the rest of our lives were good; for instance, Marvin went on a long trip around the world. Last I heard, he was on the run from the British police just for poking a king's guard. Andria became a world-famous veterinarian and helps animals everywhere; even gets into fights with poachers and trophy hunters. Talia decided to go into government and help ensure many of the corrupted still trying to seize power would never get it. Many of them tried to find something on her, but it always gave her the chance she needed to stop them. Eddy began a company of his own, which is bent on helping this planet and doing everything he could to end global warming and pollution, and ensured many historic and national parks would stay open and untouched. He even helped shut down those who wanted to keep causing horrible things like that to happen. As for me, I married Cordelia and had two daughters and a son and, like I said before, just had a peaceful life from that time forth. And now we come to the end of my story, and I do hope it has helped you know there is always a way to follow your dreams and help you find the life you are looking for. But to do this, all you have to do is listen to the right advice and believe in magic.